I0598604

FOREVER IN THE SUN

Sapphire Cay, book 6

RJ SCOTT

MEREDITH RUSSELL

Love Lane Books

Copyright

Dedication

For our family and friends

SAPPHIRE CAY 6

FOREVER IN THE *Sun*

RJ SCOTT &
MEREDITH RUSSELL

Chapter One

LUCAS DUCKED OUT OF THE WAY AND CURSED AS A PAPER plane curved back on itself and missed him by inches. Dylan was bored and he was showing his displeasure at having to wait in numerous different ways. First, he'd read the two most recent magazines; one on home design, the other a gossip rag. Then he'd gone out and bought coffee, back out to buy muffins, before disappearing to find somewhere to recycle the cups.

Usually, the most laid-back person Lucas had ever met, Dylan hated being inside and this was the result. He was a kid with nothing to do, and he was restless.

"Sorry," Dylan said. He wasn't sorry given the fact he was now making a new plane out of a sheet from the home design magazine. Lucas placed a hand over his fiancé's and stopped the making of said plane.

"He'll be back in a minute," Lucas reassured Dylan.

"You said that ten minutes ago," Dylan grumped. He sighed noisily. "What if he's back there looking at what we gave him and he thinks there is a problem?"

Lucas had heard all this before. To be honest he was just as anxious, but he couldn't afford to let himself get antsy like Dylan—he didn't think his ulcer would thank him very much for it. Instead, he was channeling his worries into being the exact opposite of how he really felt.

"Like what?" he asked in a calm, patient tone.

Dylan slumped a little and shook his head. "I don't know."

Lucas sat forward in his chair. "Oh my God," he said abruptly.

Dylan reacted with panic and sat bolt upright. "What?"

Lucas looked at Dylan. "What if they find out about my previous marriages?"

Dylan's mouth fell open and Lucas had to duck again as Dylan made to smack him upside the head. "Asshole," he muttered.

"Well, what could be a problem? Neither of us has been married before, we're both free to marry. We've done everything we need to do. This is the last thing, the license."

The door to the interior of the large dusty building opened with a resounding smack against the wall and a portly man made his way to them with an envelope in his hand. "My apologies," he began. "The photocopier jammed and I had to wait for the tech to clear it."

"No worries," Lucas lied. He took the envelope, then he and Dylan exchanged the usual pleasantries with the officer who was very excited about their marriage and what it meant for gay men everywhere. Lucas wasn't entirely sure he wanted to be an example to the world, but he nodded, agreed, and said all the right things. As they talked, Dylan edged toward the door, intent written on his features. He wanted outside, and Lucas was happy to follow.

Only when they were back outside in the sunshine did the meaning behind their visit finally sink in. The license was the last piece of their jigsaw and now nothing was stopping Dylan and him from being married. Lucas pulled Dylan into a close hug and inhaled the outdoors that clung to his lover; sun and Dylan was the best scent and Lucas wondered how he had ever managed without it before.

"Nothing stopping us now," he whispered.

Which was exactly the wrong thing to say. Dylan's cell sounded and he answered the call immediately.

"Scott? Everything okay?"

Dylan kept walking and Lucas didn't think anything of it. They were right at the start of the harbor that gave Marsh Harbor its name when abruptly Dylan stopped dead.

Shit, this can't be good. Lucas immediately went through every scenario that could involve Scott, and could stop the wedding, then quickly moved on to Adam, Scott's lover and the chef at the Cay. Had there been another incident like the oven and fire? Was Adam ill? Was it Scott?

"How much?" Dylan said incredulously. "We agreed two less than that. I don't understand how he can… damn…okay, we'll go there now…" Dylan glanced at Lucas and seemed to reconsider. "No, fuck it, we're coming home. I'll deal with him later."

Lucas waited until the call ended. Deal with whom?

Talk of money implied this was about the new boat for Sapphire Cay, which Dylan was calling *Liberty Two*. The Cay needed two boats. Lucas wasn't going to argue as it was mostly his idea to begin with. Transport to and from Sapphire Cay was Dylan's responsibility, but Lucas was the one who worked on finance and logistics. His opinion was, having two boats was better than one.

"What happened?" he asked cautiously. Dylan looked halfway between angry and resigned.

"The seller upped his price by two thousand."

Lucas's mathematical mind quickly calculated where the hell they would get that money from at short notice. He identified a couple of places before speaking again. "Can he do that?"

Dylan curled a hand into his hair. "No. Yes. I don't know."

"Would you be happy to pay the extra two?"

"We'd have to if we want that boat. Or that is what Scott told me the seller said," Dylan said immediately. "Doesn't mean I want to. Typical this shit happens just before our wedding." Dylan pressed fingers to his temples. "I don't get why everything has to be so difficult at the moment, all I want is an easy life—"

"Dylan, stop." Lucas could see Dylan winding himself up to a mini meltdown. What was wrong with his fiancé? Why was he so on edge with everything lately? Lucas was the stressy one normally. Was Dylan having second thoughts about the marriage? Dylan was the free spirit. It was Lucas who craved the *forever* to start with, but he knew Dylan had wanted marriage as much as he did.

"I can't," Dylan ground out.

"Tell me what is difficult about this? We go to the seller and negotiate. We don't have to have *that* particular boat."

Dylan leaned back against the railing by the harbor coffee shop. "I like *that* boat."

"Then we pay the extra."

Dylan shook his head. "I don't know if I like it *that* much. Two thousand." He snorted a soft laugh and blew out a breath, like he was clearing away one of the problems running around in his head. "It's fine I can look again after the wedding. Besides, we already need a new oven."

"The oven and the fire are covered by insurance," Lucas reminded him.

"And Ed sent the plans over for building the new reception area he came up with—"

"Which we budgeted for." Lucas stepped up into Dylan's space, bracketing him with his hands on the railings. "Dylan, what's wrong? Are you having second thoughts?"

"No, you were right, we need a second boat."

"Not about the boat, about us."

Dylan looked horrified, a flash of something in his blue eyes, fear or wariness, Lucas couldn't tell. "No. God, no. That's the one thing I am most sure about in my life." Dylan cradled Lucas's face with strong warm hands, and Lucas could swear there was moisture in Dylan's eyes. "I just want everything to go right so that..."

Lucas hated the tone of Dylan's voice. He sounded beaten and sad. "So that what?"

"So that you don't change your mind about marrying a

beach bum like me who drags nothing but crap around with him."

For a second Lucas was speechless. Dylan was worried about that? "I love the man I found on the Cay," he began. "And you're not a beach bum. Like it or not, you have a business and responsibilities. Hell, we even have a dog." He replayed the words. "And what exactly do you mean, crap follows you around?"

"My dad, my money, the boat, the fire in the kitchen, what else do you want me to add to the list?" Dylan stared right at Lucas, the emotion evident in his expression and filling his eyes.

"None of that is down to you, Dylan. And nothing that ever happened would scare me away."

Dylan smiled. "And I love you, Lucas. I mean, *whatever* goes wrong, I will always love you." Dylan pressed a kiss to Lucas's lips and when he deepened the kiss it was like heaven.

"Break it up, boys," Tasha called from behind them. Dylan and Lucas stood as they were for a second then separated and Lucas faced his sister. Twenty-one weeks pregnant, she was at that stage when she looked radiant, albeit a little flushed in the heat. She was in charge of a box of something that Ed had sent; cards or some such thing Ed deemed essential to the Lucas/Dylan wedding. Lucas didn't ask what Ed had sent, he just went to her side and relieved her of the square, not so heavy, package.

"You should have stayed at the Cay," Lucas admonished as she leaned against him briefly.

"Because I'm hot and waddling like a duck? I'm okay. Did you get the license?"

"Yes, and you're not waddling. You look gorgeous." Lucas hugged her briefly.

Tasha smiled up at him. "You say the nicest things, big brother, but I'm hot and tired and ready to go back now."

Dylan jumped down into the Lady Liberty. He held out a hand and between him and Lucas they assisted Tasha onto the boat. They helped to keep her steady and fussed until she was sitting as comfortably as she could under the small canopy. She'd demanded to come with them this afternoon, saying she needed to pick something up that she'd ordered herself. Lucas didn't see another package, but she was carrying a large floral bag that, for all he knew, contained the kitchen sink, it was that voluminous. Liam hadn't been overly happy with her going to Marsh Harbor but he'd backed off when his pregnant wife treated him to a discussion on why she should go and why he should stop fussing. Also, he was helping with some kind of project Jamie was working on. Lucas knew damn well Liam would be standing on the jetty waiting for them though, probably with water and fruit and an adoring expression. Lucas had never seen a man so much in love with his wife.

Now just over halfway through her pregnancy, Tasha had had her twenty-week scan. To everyone's relief, everything was as it should be. Though Lucas knew she could most likely fly if they had waited until the season ended, he was glad they had picked March for the wedding. His and Dylan's honeymoon might be the shortest honeymoon in history, with a wedding booked in only three days after theirs. But at least he didn't have to worry about Tasha, heavily pregnant on planes and boats, or the predictably unpredictable weather of the summer season. He didn't think he could have handled the stress or the worry. Slotting their wedding in the space between bookings had been the right thing to do, even if organizing it had sent Edward into some sort of wedding planner Terminator mode with such a tight deadline.

To make up for having no time after the wedding Dylan had suggested a late honeymoon to visit when she was due, but that had been nixed immediately. She was a different woman to the one who had announced she was pregnant at Christmas. She was confident and happy and said it made more sense for Lucas and his new husband to visit at the end of the Cay's off-season after the baby was born. She insisted she had all the help she needed and any time Dylan and Lucas had before the birth would be better spent on a real honeymoon, just the two of them. Lucas wasn't going to argue with his sister and Dylan talked him down off the ledge about missing the new baby's birth. Still, nothing would stop him seeing the new arrival as soon as it all happened. For now, he needed to enjoy having Tasha and Liam here for the wedding.

Dylan's dad was slowly becoming another unneeded stress for Lucas. He wondered if, in part, it was the arrival of Dylan's father two days ago, with his new wife in tow, that was contributing to Dylan getting all worked up and worried. After all, Dylan had included his dad on the list of *crap* he'd mentioned. The old man was happy with Rebecca and spent a lot of the time cornering Dylan and talking at him. Not to him. At him. About all kinds of things. Investments, the future, a family. No doubt he'd spoken of the wedding as well but one thing Dylan Senior *didn't* do was talk to Lucas much at all. He wasn't warm like he was with his new wife or Dylan.

Lucas guessed Dylan's father had things to say to him, but couldn't figure out how to say them, and so had been avoiding Lucas like the plague.

Also, the man was causing trouble here and there by wanting to be extra helpful. There had been some kind of run in yesterday between him and Adam. The upshot was that the main oven had burned circuits and the kitchen was soaked from the sprinklers. Something about Dylan's dad messing with timers and melted cheese. Lucas had tried to stay out of it for Dylan's sake, but it had taken a long time to calm Adam down, and for Scott to get Adam to rethink the wedding menu in the new parameters.

At least he could count on Edward to get the wedding under control, organizing everyone and everything. That way in four days time there would actually *be* a wedding. Lucas hoped that between now and then he didn't thump Dylan's dad, who seemed to think he knew a lot about a whole bunch of non-important things, beginning with the melting point of cheese.

"You okay?" Tasha asked. "You're in your own world."

Lucas squeezed his sister's hand. "I'm good. Thinking about the wedding, and the island, and the baby."

"Let me worry about the baby," Tasha teased. "And you focus on the wedding. The Cay can look after itself."

As the Liberty made her way toward Sapphire Cay, Lucas watched Dylan at the helm. Dylan was still the same person that Lucas fell in love with. Denim shorts and a scruffy tee, dark hair with the blond streaks just too long to be tamed, eyes so blue he could lose himself in them. Whatever obstacle they had to overcome, there were only four days to go until they were married.

Lucas was counting down the hours.

Chapter Two

"Okay, nobody panic." Dylan stood very still and held out his hands indicating for everyone to do the same. He assessed the scene in the kitchen and felt the grip of foreshadowing in his chest. He tried to push the thought from his mind. This wasn't any kind of omen. It was an accident. Today was going to be perfect. Well, almost perfect. "How did this happen? And for the love of God, please tell me Edward doesn't know?"

Adam ran his hands back through his hair and cursed under his breath. "Edward's going to kill us."

"Bloody hell and bollocks." Scott rested his hand on Adam's shoulder and smirked.

Not impressed with Scott's attempt to lighten the mood, Adam slapped away his hand. "Watch yourself or I'll tell Edward *this* is your fault." He pointed at the destroyed wedding cake.

Scott was quick to protest, "It's not my fault."

Adam didn't look convinced.

"It's nobody's fault." Dylan chewed on his lip. Or

maybe it was his. Crap. He glanced at the cake, then at Adam and Scott. They could figure something out between them, right? Scott shrugged his shoulders and Adam looked flustered.

Bollocks, indeed.

There was no time to deal with this. He was getting married in less than three hours.

"Scott, can you grab Mutt, please?"

Mutt lifted his head at the sound of his name. The dog's face was covered in white frosting, and he twisted his head as he tried to lick the sugary goodness from his snout. Shaking his head, Mutt looked up at Dylan with wide innocent eyes, a trick Dylan was sure Lucas had a hand in teaching him for getting away with, in this case, cake murder. Scott reached for Mutt, grabbing the animal by his collar and pulling him away from what was quite the massacre.

"Can we save anything?"

"Half the bottom tier. Maybe," Adam said. He nodded to what was left of the three-tier cake sitting on the trolley. From the trail of evidence, Mutt had jumped up and started on the bottom layer of the cake before knocking the pillars, collapsing the top two tiers on top of himself.

Dylan eyed the square cake. They could totally cut off the section covered in dog drool, right? Nobody would know, and it wasn't like they needed all three layers. They didn't have that many guests, not really. "Okay. I guess we could try saving it." Could they? Really? He eyed Mutt. Maybe it was best they scrapped the whole thing. If anyone was going to find a dog hair in their slice, it would be Edward. "Maybe we could..."

"What?" Adam asked.

He had no idea. "You'll think of something."

Enthusiastically, Scott suggested, "Cupcakes. We have time for those, right?"

Disbelief creased Adam's brow. "I'm going to start with B, whereby to cook, cool, and frost, what? Fifty plus cupcakes? Is not as quick and easy as you think, not when I have everything else to organize." Adam screwed his hands into fists as he spoke. "And let's go back to A, more importantly, I still don't have an oven." He raised his voice.

Scott caught his balance as Mutt lurched forward. The man wore the reprimanded schoolboy look pretty damn well. "Can you not stick them in the microwave?"

Adam opened his mouth and quickly shut it. He tilted his head as if considering the option. "No. We're not making microwave cakes." He shuddered at the sacrilegious idea Scott had put forward.

"What about Dominiq?" someone said from behind Dylan.

Dylan looked over his shoulder at Jamie. Panic gripped his chest as he searched beyond Jamie for any sign of Edward. "Where's Ed?"

"Checking strings of lights." Jamie eyed the cake on the floor. "And no, I'm not telling him about this."

Not even the super-calming effect of Edward's boyfriend would stop the wedding planner going nuclear if he found out what had happened to his beautifully designed cake.

"So what about Dominiq?" Jamie suggested again. "He wouldn't have left Marsh Harbor yet. If he hasn't time to bake, he could probably buy something as a stand in."

"Yeah, yeah. That could work." Dylan nodded with each word. They had roughly three hours to the ceremony. The ride from Marsh Harbor to the Cay was around fifty minutes. There was still time to fix all this, somehow. "Okay, marine, you're in charge of Operation Cake." He looked firmly at Jamie. "I want you to get on the phone to Dominiq and fix this mess. Whatever it takes, whatever it ends up costing me. Once you've done that, you're on Edward watch. Under no circumstances does he enter this kitchen."

Jamie nodded, turned on his heel, and headed for the office to make the call.

"Adam, you do whatever the hell it is you do. Is there anything you need? Any more staff need sending through?"

With a smile, Adam assured him everything was fine, apart from the obvious. "Everything is running to plan. Well, everything else." His gaze briefly fell to the destroyed cake. "I am so sorry."

"We can all be sorry later." Dylan flashed a smile and tried to ignore the nagging doubt he had over who was to blame. Was he supposed to have been watching Mutt?

"What about me?" Scott asked.

"You're on cleanup. Mutt, then the kitchen. I don't want Lucas finding out, so be sneaky, yeah?"

"Well, I'll try. But you know what he's like. He's almost as bad as Edward when it comes to checking on things."

That was true, and also scary. During the whole

wedding organization, it was like Dylan had been seeing double and hearing everything in stereo. Dylan would happily have turned up in board shorts on the day, married on the beach, just the two of them, and lived happily ever after. But as Edward and Lucas had reminded him, they were only going to be doing this once. Lucas deserved to have the wedding he wanted, surrounded by people who loved him.

Lucas couldn't find out about this. Not yet. He'd think it was some kind omen of doom for the rest of their day, for their future. No, today was going to be amazing and perfect and a day to remember only for good reasons. He knew what he had to do.

"It's okay. I'll just have to bring in the reinforcements," he said.

Scott quirked an eyebrow.

"Tasha."

———

THERE WAS A GENTLE KNOCK, AND LUCAS SMILED AS Tasha slowly pushed open the door.

"Are you decent?" she asked and pushed the door a little farther. "Wow." She stopped in the doorway and looked her brother up and down. "You look amazing."

Lucas took a deep breath and turned to look in the full-length mirror. "You've seen me in suits before." He had worn plenty during his years at Morgan Municipal.

"Never one on your wedding day." A smile lit her face as she moved behind him, reaching around to straighten his tie.

She was dressed in blue. A deep shade to match that of his and Dylan's ties. The short strapless dress hugged her high on her waist accentuating her full bust, then hung loose over her baby bump. Gently, she rested her hands on Lucas's shoulders and met his eyes in the mirror.

"I'm so proud of you."

Lucas turned around. "I can't believe this is really happening."

She took hold of his hand and squeezed. "I never doubted it. Dylan would do anything for you. Even settle down and stay in one place."

Lucas laughed and shook his head. "I didn't mean him."

Tasha gazed up at him. She studied his face as if looking for an answer to her unvoiced question.

"Just…a few years ago I never imagined any of this could be possible. I mean, I was working every hour of the day. That was my life. Not this." He looked down onto the beach through the open window. A warm breeze caused the light material of the drapes to blow up and carried with it the smell of ocean. Something Lucas would always associate with all the best bits of Dylan; his strong arms, his warm embrace, his smile, and his kiss. How could he have ever imagined this life? It was so far away from anything he had been living back then.

"But you're happy, right?"

With a smile, he said, "So happy." He'd been in an office working late every night, barely had any time for himself, let alone for Tasha, or to think about dating, marriage, making a real home with someone. He hadn't been living, not actually. Money and contracts had been his life, making other people rich. He had done it for Tasha and nearly worked himself into an early grave just to see her happy and financially secure. She had been his world, his everything, after their parents died. But now, she was starting her own family, had a husband who would give her the world if she asked for it. She didn't need him, not the way she used to. Lucas would never stop worrying about his baby sister. Nor would he regret the years he put into Morgan Municipal to see her through school and into a job she loved. Anyway, now it was his turn to be looked after, by a man who loved him.

"I'm hungry." Tasha rubbed her hand over her rounded stomach. She glanced at Lucas, clearly aware she had disturbed thoughts deeper than hers of food.

It wasn't just the scent of the ocean riding in on the breeze. Every now and then the smoky scent of cooking meat permeated up to the hotel as fat hit heat. With the oven out of action, Edward had suggested a hog roast on the beach—pork, rolls, potato salad. If Lucas was honest, he preferred the roast to the four-course menu Edward had worked with Adam to create. Informal was better, more them, more Dylan.

What was going through Dylan's head right then? Did he have the same butterflies in his stomach as Lucas?

In ninety minutes, he would be Mr. Madison-Gray. Or maybe Gray-Madison. Were they even doing that? The whole double-barrel thing? Or were they staying as they were? Maybe they should pick one surname. *Lucas Gray.* He chewed on his lip. *Dylan Madison.*

"Are you okay?"

Lucas nodded. He had to stop finding things to obsess

over. He'd been banned from stalking staff around and checking in with Edward every five minutes. Apparently, today was his day and it wasn't his job to worry about anything. Despite having been threatened with being locked inside his room, Lucas had snuck out to help set up the fire pit to cook the pig, then liaised with Scott over picking up guests coming into Marsh Harbor that morning. Guests including Dylan's ex Mitch and his (Lucas thought they were official) boyfriend Isaac. Others like Dominiq and his family, and various people Dylan knew off the main island, who owned boats, were making their own way to Sapphire Cay throughout the day.

Everybody he had spoken to, before being shooed to his room to relax with a breakfast of fruits and a glass of champagne, had assured him everything was going like clockwork. He just couldn't help but think that it was inevitable one of the cogs in said clock was going to wriggle itself free and cause chaos.

"Maybe I should go and make sure everyone's okay."

"Why?"

"Well, you know, they might need help with something."

"Who?" Tasha stared at him.

Lucas shrugged. "Just, people." He took her hand in his. "I want it to be perfect. I want everybody to have a good day."

"And that's what your lovely staff is here for." She smiled encouragingly. "This isn't just another wedding on the Cay. This is your wedding."

"I guess." He eyed the door. "It wouldn't hurt to check

though." He pulled his hands from hers and headed for the door.

"Oh." Tasha grabbed his elbow and nursed her stomach.

Panic gripped Lucas. "What? What is it? Are you okay? Is the baby okay?" When Tasha chuckled, his fears were allayed. "What?" He held her arm until she was seated comfortably at the end of the bed. He looked her up and down. She didn't seem worried, but he stood in front of her, waiting to hear her say the words.

"I think it's just gas." She teased her lower lip between her teeth. "Come and sit down." She patted space on the bed beside her.

Lucas glanced over his shoulder at the door, his chance for escape slipping away. With a sigh, he sat next to her. Warmth filled him as she bumped her shoulder against his, then lifted his hand into her lap.

"The last time we sat in this room together was on my wedding day. The day a certain gorgeous sun-kissed boat guy strolled into the room with a camera and stole your heart."

That day felt so long ago, but he still remembered that first sight of Dylan at the pier herding Tasha's wedding party from the airport and onto the Lady Liberty. "You looked beautiful." The same pride he had felt then surged within him. He leaned in and kissed her cheek. "Still do."

Tasha grinned. "Even with swollen ankles and bags under my eyes?"

"Especially the swollen ankles." He glanced down, light catching the diamanté jewels on the straps of her sandals.

"Not sure Liam thinks the same." She massaged her bump. "He's been amazing, listening to me complain all the time. Too hot, too cold, too fat, too swollen, too stiff. And God, the cravings."

She looked at him. Love lit her eyes. Liam was a good husband, and they were happy. Idly, she ran her hand over her plaited hair, and gently straightened the large blue flower she wore in her hair. "I actually have something for you," she said.

Lucas smiled in encouragement. She looked a little nervous.

"I was thinking about Mom and Dad and what today could have meant to them as well." She reached into a bag he hadn't spotted her bringing in and pulled out a wrapped rectangle.

He opened the wrapping gently and saw the smiling faces of his parents in a photo that was familiar to him; it had hung in his hallway as a kid for the longest time.

"Oh," he said. "Where did you find that?"

"In a box of their stuff. I was looking for that soft blanket." She smoothed a hand over her belly. "For the little one."

Lucas pulled her close in an awkward sideways hug. "Thank you."

"Do you think about them much?"

Lucas blinked, surprised by the question. "Sometimes." Most recently when Dylan was in contact with his own father. Lucas was glad the two men had managed to reach some understanding. There still some bridges to build between father and son, but things were better.

She pressed her fingers against their dad's face. "Do you think Dad would have walked you down the aisle?" Tasha pursed her lips thoughtfully. "I think he would have." She stroked her other hand over the material of her dress. "Wish they'd have gotten to meet this little dude."

"Dude?"

"Or dudette," she added. "We want it to be a surprise."

Lucas wasn't sure he could have resisted the urge to peek. "I suppose at your age you don't get many surprises anymore." He grinned when Tasha tapped his arm.

"You're such a dick."

Lucas wrapped his arm around her as she rested her chin against his shoulder. He hugged her close, narrowing his eyes as he stared at the back of the closed door. "So, are you going to tell me what's going on?"

"With what?" Tasha breathed in as she sat upright. She smiled sweetly at him.

"Gas? That was just an excuse to keep me in the room, right?"

There was no mistaking the guilt that flashed over her face.

"You are so busted." He went to stand, but Tasha held onto his hand.

"Please. Dylan told me to make sure you stayed in your room. He didn't want you worrying about anything. Not today."

As sweet as that was of Dylan, now all Lucas could imagine was worst case scenarios, most involved the Lady Liberty sitting on the bottom of the ocean with their guests still on board.

"I had one job. God I suck." She pouted.

"So are you going to tell me, or shall I go and ask Dylan?"

Tasha worried her lower lip. Eventually, she released his hand. "Fine. Sit down. You have to promise you won't freak out."

He wished he could. "I'll promise I'll *try* not to freak out."

With a huffed breath, she agreed. "Fine."

"Well?"

"Well." She faced him. "It's about your cake."

Chapter Three

"DON'T SHOW US UP. YOU GOT THAT?" DYLAN STOOD under the shade of the trees at the edge of the beach and looked down at Mutt. The dog looked back up at him, before twisting his head from side to side in an attempt to snag the blue ribbon, which held the small pale gray doggy waistcoat in place.

Dylan watched Mutt for a moment. He imagined the dog felt as overdressed and out of place as he did. Dylan didn't do suits and ties, not like this anyway. He stood tall and smoothed his hand over the material of the gray suit he wore, a similar shade to what Mutt was wearing. Why had he let Edward talk him into this?

We could always dress Adam, Scott, and Jamie in bridesmaid dresses and have them follow you down the aisle, Edward had said far too seriously.

Mutt had seemed the lesser of two evils. Besides, the dog was family now. Their boy, their baby.

With a smile, Dylan affectionately stroked Mutt's head. He stopped when he heard music echoing from the beach.

"Looks like it's time." He patted Mutt on the back and encouraged him forward with a pull on his leash.

Emerging from the trees, Dylan stopped where tufts of long grass made way for hot white sand. He glanced along the aisle. Guests were standing in front of their seats, waiting for him to make his way to the front. The lady registrar stood on a platform, beneath an arch of blue and white flowers. He wrapped the leash around his hand, keeping Mutt at his heel, as they made their way to the stage.

Dylan glanced from side to side, remembering to smile whenever he met anyone's eyes. He was relieved when he reached the front. Focusing on the area to his right, he aimed to where Scott was waiting. He handed Mutt's leash over to Scott, then took his place in front of the registrar.

Anticipation turned over his stomach and he stared back toward the trees. He wanted nothing more than to see Lucas, to touch him, to kiss him, to catch the slightest of glimpses of the man he would call husband from today. This morning had been close to torturous. He had never been one for traditions or following the rules, but Tasha had insisted they shouldn't see each other until the ceremony. He might have missed waking up with Lucas but it meant each touch and every kiss, when he did see him would be all the better for it.

The music faded into a second piece. As the instrumental recording rose in volume, so did the swell of emotions within him. He didn't think he'd ever felt so happy, nor had he ever loved someone as much as he did Lucas. He looked at his lover and couldn't help but smile.

Lucas was wearing a pale blue suit, set off with a dark

tie that matched the one Dylan wore. He looked incredible, and Dylan thought back to their first nights together, right here on the beach. Lucas had been a different man back then, they both had. Together they had grown and moved on from what their lives had been. Lucas had found a sense of peace and happiness and realized that sometimes you have to stop, take a breath, and enjoy life. And Dylan? He finally stopped running. For years he thought, if he didn't stay too long in one place, all the bad stuff and his broken relationship with his dad would get left behind and lost. The thing was, it didn't work like that. Those things he carried with him always, but with Lucas, he'd taken steps to forgive both himself and his father.

Arm in arm, Lucas and Tasha walked toward the front. Tasha was in a lightweight sapphire blue dress, tailored to fit her growing belly. Lucas lifted his head, meeting Dylan's eyes. The smile he had on his face warmed Dylan's heart and he was sure he had never felt anything like this before—pure bliss, perfect happiness, as he had everything he could ever want.

Reaching the edge of the platform, Tasha kissed her brother on the cheek and took her place on the left beside Liam. In her hands, she clutched a small posy of white flowers. The stems were wrapped tightly in blue ribbon and a small fabric purse hung from her wrist. She already seemed misty-eyed, and she leaned in close to her husband as she watched her brother with love and pride in her eyes.

Lucas stepped up to stand beside Dylan. He gently took Dylan's hands in his, then leaned forward. "I know," he whispered and pressed a kiss to Dylan's jaw.

Dylan looked at his fiancé and narrowed his eyes. "What?" he mouthed.

"Cake," Lucas mouthed in return.

There was no chance to reply as the music faded and the registrar welcomed them and their guests. He half-listened to her words, all the time his attention firmly on his soon-to-be husband. If Lucas was upset about the cake, he wasn't showing it. He looked happy. Briefly, their gaze met and Lucas reassuringly squeezed Dylan's hands. The cake didn't matter. What mattered was they were here, they were together, and they were about to seal their happy ever after with vows and the exchanging of rings.

And that was everything to Dylan.

***

Dylan looked directly at Lucas, and as he spoke his voice was soft, but he didn't hesitate once in what he said.

"Lucas, you changed my life. You made me a better person. You *make* me a better person. I never thought I would find that, and I will love you as my husband every single day for the rest of our lives, if you let me."

Lucas caught his breath as Dylan finished his promise. He smiled. "I will. I do." Dylan pushed the wedding band down his finger and into place. Lucas eyed the metal as it caught the sun.

"And Lucas." The registrar moved the service on.

Lucas took the second ring from Scott. Squeezing his hand into a ball, he tried to fight his nerves. Though writing their own vows sounded romantic, it was so damn stressful. Was what he had written too long, too short? Was it over-sentimental or too generic?

His hand was shaking as he held the ring over the tip of Dylan's finger. He looked at Dylan, reassured when Dylan gave him a comforting smile.

"Dylan Joseph Gray. You are the most beautiful, generous soul I have ever met. You bring the sunshine into my life every day, and that's saying something, considering we live in a paradise." He paused, losing himself for a moment in the warmth of Dylan's hand as he held onto it. "I don't know what kind of person I would be if I hadn't met you. You could quite possibly have saved my life." He swallowed hard. "You bring out the best in me, and I love you. Even when you trail sand into our bedroom, and it gets everywhere." Dylan laughed. His smile lit his face and Lucas felt so damned light he thought he would float away. "So, with this ring, I promise to make every day together special, to live life and make it count. I will love you until we're old and sea-weathered, until we're sand on the breeze. Be my husband."

Dylan nodded. "Yes."

Relieved, Lucas pushed the ring over Dylan's knuckle. He then grasped Dylan's hands in his.

"You are now husband and husband. Congratulations." The registrar raised her hands and gave them a nod. This was their moment.

They leaned in, their hands still entwined at their sides as they kissed one another. Closing his eyes, Lucas breathed in the familiar scent of home, of the ocean, of his man. Blinking, he opened his eyes, and they parted. They stood hand in hand and faced their guests, who were on their feet applauding them. Lucas glanced at his sister. Tears glistened on her cheeks as she beamed happily. Dylan squeezed his hand, and he turned to him. He let out a contented sigh as Dylan kissed him again.

When Dylan pulled away, Lucas licked his lips, tasting the kiss. He looked at the friends and family with whom they were sharing this moment. The start of their forever.

LUCAS LEANED BACK AGAINST DYLAN AS THEY LAY ON THE beach. The sun was low in the sky as the evening drew in on a beautiful day. Dylan's father stood over them.

"Beautiful ceremony," he said.

"Thank you, Dad," Dylan said. He scrambled to stand and father and son embraced. When they separated both were smiling.

"You think I could get a few minutes with your new husband?"

Dylan looked down at Lucas and extended a hand and helped him up. "Be nice," he joked. Although given he was talking to his husband and his father he wasn't fooling anyone that he didn't have worry in his voice.

Lucas walked with his new father-in-law a little way from the main celebration, and at some point Dylan Senior deemed appropriate, he stopped and turned to face Lucas.

"I wanted to talk to you," he said.

That sounded ominous. Lucas braced himself for something bad.

"I thought you might." Lucas was happy to say that he'd noticed Dylan's father avoiding him.

"I wanted to say sorry, and to thank you."

"Thank me for what?" Lucas attempted to sound like he wasn't suspicious. Was that a sarcastic thank you, or a genuine one?

"For taking such good care of Dylan's heart. Is all." Dylan Senior looked uncomfortable, like every part of him was open and vulnerable with those simple words. "I wanted to say the minute we arrived, then I realized I just sounded like a damn idiot." He looked down at his shoes then back at Lucas.

"And I wanted to say thank you as well," Lucas said.

Dylan Senior raised a single eyebrow in a mannerism Lucas had grown used to seeing on Dylan's expression. That moment of skepticism, or worry, or surprise, all summed up in one perfect raised arch.

Lucas carried on, "Thank you for coming to the wedding, and for allowing Dylan to try and build bridges, and for Dylan himself. I love your son and I will always be there for him."

Dylan's father nodded before extending his hand.

Lucas went to shake it, but instead bypassed that and went straight in for a hug. The hug was awkward, stiff at first, then Dylan's dad relaxed into the hold. They patted each other on the back and separated, both grinning like idiots.

"I must go and find Rebecca," Dylan Senior said with a smile.

Lucas watched him leave, saw the way he swung Rebecca into his arms, then decided to find his own man. He slumped back on the sand next to Dylan.

"Okay?" Dylan asked.

"Yeah. Very okay."

Idly, he curled his fingers around Dylan's, smiling when Dylan reciprocated the gentle touches. He looked at the fire burning on the beach, and at the people standing around it. Some were talking, others swaying to the low music echoing down from the hotel patio, and some interactions seemed a little more intimate. He smiled, feeling peaceful. Turning his head, he eyed the tree line and the strings of white lights, which faded in and out in a steady rhythm. Edward had outdone himself once again.

"So, cake?" Edward appeared behind them and crouched down in the sand. He raised his hands as if the grains of white would burn him, and started brushing at his pant leg. "What the hell happened?"

Laughing, Lucas leaned back his head. No way was he explaining this one. Nobody had told Edward. Somehow Jamie had managed to run Operation Cake, as Dylan had teasingly declared the events of earlier, like some covert mission. Lucas had no idea how Edward had been convinced to stay away from the kitchen, and found Edward wide-eyed and confused when the new makeshift wedding cake had been rolled out for the newlyweds to cut.

Clearing his throat, Dylan just said, "Mutt."

"I always said that the dog had it in for me."

Lucas grinned.

"Dominiq did the best he could at short notice. To be honest I was really impressed." Dylan somehow managed to remain straight-faced.

"Impressed, huh?" Lucas looked up at Dylan.

Edward raised a dark eyebrow above the frame of his

glasses. "Pink and yellow frosting?" he said of the cupcakes Dominiq had brought over to the island. "The color scheme was blue."

Lucas and Dylan both looked at Edward and couldn't stop themselves from laughing.

"It's not funny," Edward insisted.

"It's a little funny." Lucas rested his hand on Edward's knee. "It's just frosting."

"Whatever," Edward said, and stared at Dylan. "And the less we say about your other *cakes*, the better."

When Adam had wheeled out the trolley, he must have apologized a dozen times. The cupcakes had been set around the edge of the cart, framing the slightly wonky, and rather mismatched three tiers of their improvised wedding cake. The base had been a plain white iced cake. The middle layer had been in the shape of a castle, a small princess and knight sitting on the corner of what was clearly a children's birthday cake. At the top had been a chocolate sponge covered in a thick layer of chocolate frosting and dark chocolate shavings. All Lucas could think to say at the time was how unique it was. Hideous, but different, and sometimes different was good.

"At least they tasted okay," Dylan pointed out.

Edward heaved a breath. "Thank heaven for small mercies."

"Are you still going on about those cakes?" Jamie dropped down on the sand beside Edward and quickly received a telling off about getting sand all over him. "Yeah, yeah." Jamie wrapped his arms around Edward and pulled him to him, toppling the wedding planner until his ass hit the beach. "Oops."

Lucas smirked. Jamie was a braver man than him, or just too drunk to care.

"Let's dance," Jamie said and pulled on Edward's arm. He gave a lazy smile. "Come on. You're off the clock now, right?"

Edward sighed, leaned over and kissed Jamie, then excused them. "Have a great night." He got to his feet. He glanced down at the sand clinging to his clothes. For a moment, it looked like he was going to wipe at the material of his pants. Lucas could imagine the poor man spending countless hours after visiting the Cay obsessively shaking and dusting down his clothes. But right then, the need to be with his lover was enough to break the spell. Seeming to make peace with clinging sand, Edward wrapped his hand around Jamie's and guided him toward the fire where they joined the other couples moving in time to the music.

"Would you like to dance?" Dylan asked, having noticed Lucas watching Edward and Jamie.

Gently, Lucas folded down his fingers, then pulled Dylan's hand to his lips. "I'm okay. Just thinking."

"About?"

"Whether it's too early to make our escape." He looked up at Dylan. He rested his head against Dylan's chest and grinned. "Do you think anyone would notice if we slipped away?"

A smirk teased the corner of Dylan's mouth. "Not if we were quick."

Lucas considered the people on the beach. Full of food and alcohol, people were happy to relax and talk in small groups. Nobody would notice if they disappeared for a little while. "Not too quick though, right?" He leaned forward as Dylan sat upright.

"D." The familiar nickname was called from farther down the beach.

Dylan raised a hand, waving when he spotted Mitch and Isaac heading in their direction. "They're coming over," he said to Lucas through gritted teeth.

"I can see that."

"What do we do?"

"Smile." Lucas forced a smile as the couple reached them. "Hi," he said. "You guys having fun?" He cursed himself for the feigned enthusiasm as Mitch gave him an odd look.

"It's lovely." Isaac looked over his shoulder at the fire. "It reminds me of the shoot we did here."

"Oh yes. How did the launch go?" Dylan asked.

Lucas shot him a wide-eyed look. Dylan wasn't supposed to be making conversation.

"It was brilliant," Mitch said and sat down.

Lucas resisted the urge to groan, instead choosing to sulk in silence. He stared at the fire, then looked up at Isaac, who had opted to stay standing. He met Lucas's eyes, a curiosity sparking in them.

Did he realize what plans they had interrupted?

"Were you two going somewhere?" He directed the question at Lucas in a quiet voice, ducking his head as he glanced at Dylan and Mitch.

Dropping his shoulders, Lucas shook his head and invited Isaac to sit down. "No. No. Of course not." He smiled a genuine smile and caught Dylan's gaze.

"I love you," Dylan mouthed, briefly turning his attention from Mitch.

Lucas's smile widened. He would look forward to being shown exactly how much Dylan loved him later. For now, they had guests who had taken time out to share this day with them. The least they could do was stick around for a while, as tempting as getting Dylan alone and naked was right then.

Dylan and Mitch had slipped into an easy conversation, probably about the good old days. Lucas glanced at Isaac. He didn't really know the man. Only what he knew from when they were on the island for the fashion shoot. What the hell could they talk about?

In the end, it was Isaac who broke the silence between them. "So, your cake?"

"Yeah." Lucas relaxed.

"It was a little unusual."

Grinning, Lucas turned to face Isaac and said, "Yeah. It was." *And it was perfect.*

Chapter Four

"Fuck. I've wanted you all night." Dylan wrapped his hands under Lucas's thighs and lifted him from the ground. He pushed his husband back against the side of the cabin, eliciting a groan from Lucas as his back hit the hard wall.

"Want you so bad." Lucas had his hands on Dylan's shoulders, gripping him tightly as he aided Dylan in keeping his feet off the ground.

Dylan kissed Lucas with a sense of urgency. He couldn't wait to get Lucas inside and into bed. He was drunk and horny. So freaking horny. Every time he had caught Lucas's eye that evening, the other man's heated gaze had sent desire straight to Dylan's dick. He was hard and wanted in Lucas right-the-hell now.

Teasingly, he rotated his hips in the space between Lucas's legs, driving his lover wild.

"Asshole," Lucas uttered. "You're going to bring me off right here if you're not careful." He moved his hands to

Dylan's jaw, cupping his face as he pulled him into a passionate kiss.

Their lips met in a rough kiss. Lucas sucked and nipped at Dylan's lips, before opening his mouth and flicking out his tongue. Dylan welcomed Lucas inside. With a soft sigh, he sucked on Lucas's tongue. Lucas tasted sweet, like one of the fruity cocktails he had been drinking that evening.

"I love you," Dylan murmured into the kiss.

Lucas leaned back and licked his kiss-plumped lips. He drew his lower lip between his teeth and smiled. "Show me."

Dylan grinned. "Key?"

They were standing outside the private cabin at the south of the island. It meant their guests could carry on the party while they had a little *them* time.

Lucas managed to lift his hip in Dylan's hold and freed the key from his pocket. Teasingly, he ran the key down Dylan's chest, pulled the key back when Dylan went to take it, and instead captured Dylan's mouth in another kiss. Lucas ran his fingers through Dylan's hair and held him close.

Kissing was good. Desire swelled inside Dylan, and he could feel the strain of his erection in the front of his dress pants. He reached up, grabbing Lucas by his wrists, and pressed them to the side of the cabin. He leaned back a little, still angling his body to keep Lucas off the ground. "Key," he said with a firm growl.

Lucas visibly squirmed at the demand and let the key hang loosely between his index finger and thumb.

Releasing Lucas's wrists, he snatched the key before

Lucas could tease him further, then lowered him to the floor. He unlocked the door and held out his hand. He smiled when Lucas took it. Dylan looked his husband up and down. Husband. This was real. They'd really done it.

Gently, he pulled on Lucas's arm, guiding him inside. As soon as the door closed behind them, they wasted no time in picking up where they had left off. Dylan flicked on the light and moved forward, wrapping his hands around the back of Lucas's head and kissing him hard. He forced Lucas back against the door. The impact of their bodies shook the cabin wall and made the glass in the door rattle.

Sighing, Lucas leaned his head back, allowing Dylan access to more skin as he nuzzled his mouth against the side of Lucas's throat.

Dylan kissed and sucked at Lucas's neck hard enough to mark him, all the time pressing his palm to the front of Lucas's pants. He licked a line upward, grazing his teeth against Lucas's chin before drowning out Lucas's sounds of arousal with a kiss. With one hand, he held Lucas's head steady, and with the other, he eased inside Lucas's clothes and cupped his dick through the material of his boxer briefs.

"Fuck," Lucas groaned out.

Dylan reached lower and slipped his fingers up the leg of Lucas's underwear. He met Lucas in an open-mouthed kiss and teased the man's erection from beneath the material. He kissed Lucas and circled the head of Lucas's dick with his index finger and thumb. Nipping at Lucas's lip, he made short firm strokes of Lucas's cock. The sounds his husband made ignited the need for more.

"Bedroom?"

"Uh-huh," Lucas managed.

Another firm kiss and Dylan pulled away. He stood for a moment, drinking in the sight of his husband. His blond hair had been disheveled by Dylan's eager touch, his lips were plumped and pink from Dylan's rough kisses, and his amber eyes seemed to be aglow with emotion. He looked happy, content. Like he'd gotten everything he ever wanted. Lucas looked incredible.

Lucas is *incredible.*

"How did I get so lucky?" Dylan hadn't meant to say it out loud and he lowered his eyes when Lucas tilted his head in curiosity.

Damn. Dylan cursed his words and how they had stalled the moment.

Lucas stepped forward. His attention settled on Dylan's loose necktie, and he seductively ran it through his fingers and thumb. "Nothing to do with luck. Some things are just meant to be." He wrapped the tie around his hand and pulled.

Dylan tensed against Lucas's tug and locked eyes with him as Lucas pulled himself close. "I love you."

Lucas smirked. "Are you sure?"

"Of course."

"I'm not so sure." Lucas shook his head and placed a kiss to Dylan's mouth. He looked at Dylan through his lashes. "I guess you'll have to show me."

"I'll show you." He pulled Lucas into a firm kiss and turned him around.

In between kisses, they undressed and made their way through to the bedroom. Dylan moved Lucas backward with purpose. They reached the end of the bed, and Dylan pushed Lucas back onto the mattress.

Lucas stared up at him. His mouth was wet and inviting, and before Dylan could imagine Lucas's mouth wrapped around his dick, sucking him off, it was happening.

"Fuck." He leaned back his head and stared up at the light. Lucas's mouth felt damn good. Dropping his head forward, Dylan watched his husband work his mouth around his dick. Lucas alternated between shallow and deep sucks. First he teased the head of Dylan's dick, circling his tongue around the tip, and licking a line down his shaft. He took Dylan's full length inside his mouth for several firm bobs of his head.

"Oh God." The tip of his dick hit the back of Lucas's throat. At the same time, Lucas moved his hand under his balls, pressing against them with the palm of his hand, before caressing a line toward his ass.

He reached down and ran his fingers through Lucas's hair. He smiled at the sensation of Lucas's soft locks brushing over the back of his hands. Pleasure tightened his stomach muscles, and he curled his fingers down. "Gonna," he uttered. "Gonna come."

At the declaration, Lucas reached around and grabbed Dylan's ass cheeks firmly. He buried his head in Dylan's crotch, holding him close as he hollowed his cheeks, and applied pressure with each suck of Dylan's dick.

"Oh." Dylan's body shook as his climax hit. He couldn't help but thrust forward, deeper into Lucas's mouth. Lucas continued to suck hard, milking every last drop of his release and swallowing it down. "Fuck," Dylan said breathlessly. He twitched as Lucas released his dick, then licked a line down his softening shaft.

"I fucking love you." He leaned down and kissed Lucas. The taste of himself on Lucas's lips excited him and he needed to be in Lucas. He wanted to bring his husband to the edge and fall into pure bliss alongside him.

Lucas grinned and rested his hands on Dylan's waist, as he leaned in to press kisses to Dylan's stomach.

"Lie down," Dylan instructed between harsh breaths. He needed Lucas to be where he was, to feel what he had, to lose it like Dylan was his everything.

Lucas looked up at him and pressed his mouth into a seductive pout. "Okay." Leaning back, he slowly moved to the top end of the bed. "I came up here last night." He looked at the nightstand. "In the drawer." Lucas said. His voice was gravelly, and lust overwhelmed Dylan.

Excitement tightened in Dylan's stomach as he found the lube and condoms. Quickly, he was at Lucas's side, kneeling, and held out the lube to Lucas. "You do it."

Lucas sat up on his knees, taking the lube with a kiss. He coated his fingers and reached behind him.

Dylan grabbed Lucas's other wrist and pulled him close, pressing their chests together as he kissed him. He gripped Lucas's arm tightly and squeezed the flesh of Lucas's hip with his other. Lucas arched his body, pressed his fingers into himself, and Dylan kissed him soundly. Passion tightened in Dylan's chest as he opened his mouth, allowed Lucas in. They worked their tongues around each other's, and Dylan breathed in the soft gasps as Lucas readied himself.

Desire had Dylan's dick so fucking hard he wanted in

Lucas. He wanted to fuck every pleasurable sound of love and want out of his man. Releasing Lucas's wrist, he grabbed Lucas round the back of the head and deepened the kiss. The moment was rough, his carnal passion raging inside him as he reached behind Lucas and slid his finger alongside Lucas's.

Lucas fought against Dylan's hold on him, managing to break the kiss as Dylan pressed his fingertip inside. "Fuck," he gasped and leaned his head back. He made soft sounds as Dylan fucked their fingers back and forth together and nuzzled his neck.

Dylan breathed in deeply and flicked his tongue against the mark he had left.

Mine.

"Ready?" he mumbled against Lucas's neck.

"Yeah. Fuck yeah." Lucas made a throaty sound as Dylan released him.

Dylan rolled the condom down his dick as Lucas lay down on his back. Shuffling lower, Lucas raised his legs and spread them wide, inviting Dylan into the space between them. Dylan leaned over Lucas and kissed him. Taking his dick in his hand, Dylan rubbed it back and forth down the line of Lucas's body until he found the slick dip of his entrance. He pushed forward, eliciting a groan from Lucas as he eased inside.

"Fuck." Lucas gasped, as he reached above his head, holding onto the back of the bed.

Dylan savored each inch as he moved deeper inside. He kept things slow. With each steady thrust, he pushed deeper, his thighs eventually flush with Lucas's ass as he leaned over for another kiss. He rotated his hips, settling deep in the space. Delicately, he gripped Lucas's lower lip between his teeth, drawing back slightly before releasing it, and kneeling back. The sight of Lucas beneath him sent a surge of heat through him, and he suddenly felt desperate. He thrust forward.

Lucas gripped the top of the low headboard tightly, his eyes locked with Dylan's. His mouth fell open in a muted gasp with each of Dylan's powerful thrusts.

Dylan smiled. He wanted more. He wanted Lucas to have more, to have all of him. He hooked his arm under Lucas's knee, lifting his leg until Lucas's calf rested on his shoulder. He twisted his body in the wider space and moved his hips from side to side as he buried himself deeper with each bump of his body to Lucas's. It felt so good. Dylan gripped Lucas by his ankle, pushing Lucas's leg forward toward the wall, and he held Lucas's shoulder with his other hand. Finding the leverage he needed, Dylan set his pace. He looked down at his husband and he was overwhelmed with love. The same love they had shared from the beginning. It was beautiful.

Dylan closed his eyes. He could detail every line of Lucas's incredible body and handsome face. Lucas was his everything, his forever. He opened his eyes when he sensed Lucas's hand between them. Dylan watched the changes in Lucas's features as he touched himself. The curve of his mouth, the flush of color in his cheeks as he tensed with each of his own strokes. The way his eyes became glassy, shining with the same joy Dylan felt on every one of his thrusts. Dylan curled his hand around Lucas's on the headboard, briefly quickening his pace as he sensed the tension in both their bodies. He eased his rhythm. He wanted them to come together. The pressure building in his balls was so intense. He wasn't sure he'd last.

Lucas arched his hips up off the bed. He thrust his ass down hard on Dylan's cock. Then, he came, coating his stomach in white heat. "Guh."

Dylan lost it. He held onto Lucas's leg, grazing his teeth against goose-pimpled skin as he muted his cry. He squeezed his eyes shut and fucked out his orgasm until he could stand no more. Breathless, he released Lucas's ankle and waited for him to settle both his legs on the mattress.

Lucas looked up at him. He smiled then leaned back against his pillow. "Kiss me."

Dylan curled his mouth thoughtfully as he stared down at his husband.

What did I ever do to deserve you?

Doing as Lucas requested, Dylan leaned down and planted a firm kiss on his mouth. He laughed as Lucas wriggled his ass, causing a strange sensation to shoot to Dylan's groin. Dylan kissed him again, taking a moment to just *be* with Lucas.

You are my everything.

Reluctantly, he leaned back and reached between them. They both let out a grunt as Dylan pulled out. He caught his breath and leaned down for more kisses. He ran his fingers over Lucas's jaw and gently teased down his lower lip with his thumb.

"I love you." He must have said that a hundred times that evening.

Lucas smiled and pressed his lips to Dylan's.

You are my happy ever after.

Chapter Five

"YOUR TWO O'CLOCK IS HERE, MR. FRENCH." MIRIAM'S voice floated in over the intercom. The abruptness of it startled Connor from his cost-benefits analysis and he knocked his coffee down, sloshing it onto the paperwork.

"God dammit," he muttered under his breath. He couldn't get the figures to balance and trying to find a missing ten-dollar transaction in among a million dollar bank account was screwing with his head. Where had three hours gone? He glanced sideways at his lunch. Or what was left of it. He was surprised he'd managed to actually eat at all because he certainly didn't remember the food arriving or him even picking up the ham on rye. He had to get these reports done before the accounts department could sign off on them.

He pressed the button. "Give me two," he said.

Quickly he scooped the plate, with the remaining food, into his top drawer and straightened enough paperwork to look efficient. He didn't recall the details of this two o'clock, just that it was someone with issues about the Foundation. Connor was used to answering all kind of questions, from students, politicians, kids to teachers and there was no one at this Foundation who knew what type of work they undertook as well as him. Apart from Miriam, who had been a PA at the Foundation longer than Connor had been alive. She knew where all the bodies were buried and Connor would be lost without her.

A knock on the door heralded the visitor's arrival and Connor stood, brushing his shirt of crumbs as he called, "Come in."

The door opened and Connor had to stop his mouth falling open. *Gorgeous. Very nice.* Tall, slim, dark hair, with added sexy smile and confidence in the way he walked in. Connor checked him out, couldn't help it, he hadn't seen anything this *fine* in a very long time. *I need to get out more*. From head to toe, his gaze finally focused back on the man's face and embarrassment washed over him when the guy was looking at him with one eyebrow raised in question. So much for subtle. *Well, at least he isn't punching me to the floor*.

Connor coughed away his embarrassment and held out a hand, staring into intriguing light blue eyes. "Connor French," he said. The other man shook his hand.

"Shaun Jamieson. Thank you for seeing me, Mr. French."

"Call me Connor."

Shaun inclined his head, "Shaun, then," he replied.

Connor was having difficulty placing Shaun. He was too old to be a student journalist and had to be around Connor's age. He was too casual in the way he was dressed, in jeans and a loose blue T-shirt, to be a teacher or professional politician. Maybe he was a social worker. Connor had plenty of interaction with family services during the Foundation's work with inner-city kids.

"Please take a seat." Shaun placed a file on the desk in front of him then took the proffered chair and, as soon as he was sitting, Connor sat back as well.

"Can I get you a coffee or something?"

"No, thank you, I'm all right," Shaun answered.

"I apologize, but the meeting didn't give any details of what you'd like to talk about. May I ask what the French Foundation can do for you?"

Shaun leaned forward a little in his chair. "It's not so much the French Foundation itself," he began. "It's more of a personal project I need help with."

Ahh, Connor thought, it's going to be one of *those* meetings. He couldn't understand why Miriam had allowed Shaun in if all he wanted was to push some project that needed money. Typically personal projects that needed funding never made it past the door without the admin department checking the proposals out. "We have project managers to assess financial allocations," Connor said firmly. "You need to book an appointment with the second floor and they'll be able to assist you."

Shaun frowned, then smiled, "Oh, I'm not here for money," he said brightly. "Just information. I'd like to talk to you about Peter French."

Connor's head hurt. He'd left his glasses at home and

strained his eyes, and the words that were leaving Shaun's mouth had his shields rising immediately. Shaun couldn't be here to talk about the great *family secret*. That would just be a crazy coincidence given the stand up row he'd had with his grandfather over the subject of things that usually weren't spoken of. Family secrets being one thing; Connor being gay the other thing.

"Had this letter, asking about things that shouldn't be talked about. You get any contact from anyone and you don't tell them a thing. Bad enough we have someone sniffing about without exposing things that should remain hidden. This will kill Annalisa. I saw her heart broken once, and I won't let it happen again."

"Sorry?" Connor said. Shaun needed to clarify what he was asking, and waiting to have to answer gave Connor breathing space. He'd promised his grandfather that no family secrets would be spilled, even if he was smarting at yet another personal attack for him being gay.

Gay, just like Peter had been. Peter French, the man who had, according to Connor's grandfather, nearly destroyed the family.

Shaun opened the folder, taking out a photo and placing it on the desk, shuffling it so it faced the right way to Connor. "This is Peter French."

Connor nodded. He'd seen the photo before, taken in the seventies with requisite broad collars and a fat purple tie. It had been taken at some kind of prize-giving event and the original photo was in the gallery that ran down the corridor in this building. Maybe this was all a cosmic coincidence. Shaun didn't necessarily need to be here about what had happened in the thirties and forties, he could really just be here asking questions about the history of this place and the good work it had done. Connor attempted to stay polite and push his grandfather's words out of his head.

"What do you want to know?" Connor asked. "We have a leaflet on the roots of the Foundation and the part that Peter French played in that. Miriam will be happy to give the information to you."

Shaun frowned. "No, I was after something more than that." Shaun pulled out another photo, this time of a much younger Peter standing next to a woman who Connor recognized immediately.

A fondness welled inside Connor. "Aunt Annalisa," he said. "Where did you get this? I don't think I've seen this photo before."

Shaun didn't answer that question. "Annalisa Bainbridge has refused to speak to me, or rather Oscar French, your grandfather, has threatened to sue me if I approach her again."

Connor looked up from the photo to Shaun. Gorgeous sexy Shaun who all of a sudden became someone he didn't want in his office. "Sorry?" he said again. Seemed like all his business experience of how to deal with awkward meetings had deserted him.

"I'm writing a book, about Peter and his lover Alfie, and I'd like to talk to Annalisa."

Connor's world tilted and shock quickly followed. "You need to leave now," he said. His protective instinct toward an aunt he loved had him fired up. He'd been tasked with shutting down these rumors by his grandfather. Though there had been an urgency in wanting to get him out to the middle of fucking nowhere to get a pile of old letters, it had never been so great as to have him drop everything. The content of those letters was between the French family and the men who had found them. They had no idea who Alfie was or how to contact any relations if there were any. Hell, Connor hadn't known until he'd brought the letters to the attention of his grandfather. So Connor didn't understand. Who was this stranger coming into his office, claiming to know details of something he shouldn't? Nobody else was supposed to know there was an Alfie. Oscar French had told Connor to protect Annalisa by all means, but Connor hadn't really understood what that meant until Shaun had waltzed in and made it all real.

Connor stood abruptly, and Shaun copied him slower and more deliberate. "All I want is to talk. There are letters—"

"I think you should go now. The Foundation has no comment to make."

Shaun held out a hand. "Wait, I want to write this in collaboration with the Foundation—"

"Do I need to call security?"

"You don't get it, I want to write the real story, the love story, about what it was like to be gay in pre-war America—"

Connor balled his hands into fists and pressed them on his desk. His grandfather's threats and fears and his love for Annalisa were behind every word. "You write a damn sensationalist word about *that*, and I'll get our entire team of our lawyers on your back."

Shaun pursed his lips and a stubborn expression

washed away the polite smiles. "This is the twenty-first century, Mr. French, it's okay to be gay, you know."

Connor very deliberately pressed the button on the intercom. "Miriam, can you call security, and get the lawyers on line one for me."

"Yes, Mr. French."

Shaun shook his head. He looked exasperated. "I don't get this shit," he muttered. Then he gathered together the photos and pushed them in the folder before placing a small card on the desk. "Don't worry, I'm going." He opened the door and at the last minute he turned and said, "My number is on that card if you change your mind."

The door shut behind him and Connor moved to the window, waiting until he saw Shaun Jamieson walk out of the building and onto the street three stories below. He couldn't see Shaun's expression, but the man's body posture screamed anger.

"Do you want to tell me why I had to get the lawyers on the line?" Miriam said from the door behind him.

"Shaun Jamieson, asking questions I'm not allowed to answer." Connor turned to face Miriam.

"What kind of questions?"

Connor looked at Miriam. She most likely knew more than he did. "About Peter French."

"What about him?"

"That whole thing on the island when he was young."

"With that Alfie Jamieson?" As she spoke Alfie's name, a light dawned in her eyes. "I never... That was so long ago, the whole affair buried. So I guess it's more than a coincidence he has the same surname as Peter French's lover, then?"

"How did you let him in?"

Miriam checked her ever-present notebook. "Shaun Jamieson, and no, I didn't see the connection. He's a journalist, spoke to me last week saying he would like to interview you. No red flags." She crossed to the same window and looked down into the street. Connor hadn't put two and two together about the name in his diary, which proved how screwed his head was. "I never thought he was here about Annalisa and Peter."

Miriam crossed to the phone and in smooth tones canceled the call to the lawyer's department. Then she sighed heavily. "Well, he's gone now. I'll see what I can find out about him."

"Don't worry. I'll look him up." Connor waited until she'd left before sitting back at his desk.

Google returned several results that seemed to match the man who had stood in his office. A journalist, a writer, there wasn't much else to be found on the Internet. There weren't any photos, and Facebook threw up nothing that matched. Very deliberately he closed Google and pushed all thoughts of Shaun out of his head. He needed to focus on the figures. Miriam was right, Shaun was gone and Connor had closed the questions down.

But will he stay away? There had been determination in the man's pale blue eyes. A stubbornness and focus in them that meant he was probably not gone at all.

Connor supposed it didn't matter. His cell rang and he picked it up and answered it as soon as he saw the name on the screen.

"Gramps," he said.

"Miriam just called me."

"It's nothing to worry about," Connor said immediately.

"I don't want him printing a God damn thing," Oscar said. He wasn't shouting, yet, but he was strident with evident frustration.

"I'll inform the lawyers," Connor said.

"I'm getting Miriam to clear your diary. You need to get to that damn island and shut this down once and for all. The man there says he has proof of what Peter did, proof that he could hand to that journalist."

"I know, but—"

"I've told you this will break Annalisa and she's not getting any younger." Annalisa Bainbridge was ninety-five and was fit and active. Connor wasn't going to argue on this point when he had the bigger picture to look at. Yet again he was allowing his grandfather to tell him what to do. But he loved Annalisa. The thought of her being hurt...

"None of it will get back to Annalisa. I promise you."

"She'd be devastated."

"I know, Gramps."

"And I want you to be very sure everything is gone."

"I promise you."

"Good. Good." Just as suddenly as he had phoned, Oscar French dropped the call, leaving Connor staring at numbers in a kind of blank daze. Which clearly was the best state of mind to be in when he noticed the ten-dollar discrepancy immediately.

All of this family crap, his Gramps all uptight, Annalisa's happiness at stake, but Connor could abruptly focus on a tiny amount in a sea of numbers.

Go figure.

He saved the file and sat back in his chair, opening the bottom drawer of his desk and pulling out the sealed bag of papers that formed what was left of Peter. A journal, and some detailed drawings of shells he liked to think were by Peter's hand. There were a couple of letters. This was all that the French family had left of Peter and when Oscar had dumped them in Connor's lap, he hadn't held back with his opinions on gay men and war.

Connor hadn't read any of it so far. Perhaps now was the time to get some kind of understanding for who Peter was.

Chapter Six

SHAUN BOOKED HIS LUGGAGE IN AND JUDGED HE HAD ninety minutes to kill before the flight. He had his notes to go through, drafts of questions he wanted to ask, and the two-day nagging disappointment to wrestle with that he hadn't gotten any further with fleshing out who Peter French had been. Damn French family had closed all the doors to him. Annalisa wouldn't speak to him apparently, or so Oscar said. As to Oscar French, nephew of Peter, well he'd refused to see him. Now, Connor French, youngest of the family had reacted exactly as Shaun suspected he would.

It's not like I'm some kind of tabloid hack. He'd gone into the French office two days ago with a whole slew of reasons why the French family had nothing to fear from a book that detailed a life so many years ago.

He'd had the rationale about why he wanted to know more about his own great-grandfather's youth. About the stories that had been passed down through the generations. Until the legacy of what society had made Alfie Jamieson have to hide was exposed. He stopped at the first coffee shop he could find and ordered the strongest coffee they had, before sitting in the corner with his back to the wall, facing out to people watch.

All he'd managed to get out was that it was the twenty-first century and no one gave a shit. Well, no one that was educated and actually mattered. Why was he only able to get that much out? He groaned and felt like burying his head in his hands. Fucking Connor French had checked Shaun out, Shaun was convinced of it. Somehow in those few seconds there had been an unspoken connection between two gay men in the same room, both of whom found the other attractive. Of course Connor wouldn't have seen Shaun checking Connor out because he was too busy tracking his gaze from toes to eyes and back again. That simple connection had sent way too much blood south instead of it circulating oxygen to his damn brain.

What a fucking shame. Connor was his type, all that buttoned-down goodness wrapped in a suit, pristine and pressed, ready to be unwrapped.

So you lost it, you idiot. You let a beautiful face pull you off the agenda you had in your head. He'd blown it, the shutters fell, and there was no damn way he was going to get any information from Connor.

The whole visit to the Foundation itself had been a last ditch attempt to get cooperation, and now he had one thing to rely on. Sapphire Cay and Dylan Gray.

Just like he had been doing since he'd first emailed Dylan, he pulled up the Sapphire Cay website. This was the island where Peter French fell in love with Alfie Jamieson. The place was paradise, an island in the

Bahamas, stunning white-gold sand, shallow blue waters, palm trees, full fuchsia flowers and rooms with windows open to the sea. There was an on-site chef, pool, a cocktail hut, and though he was going to be on the island as a guest, he still had to pay for his flight.

Authors didn't make much money, or at least he didn't, yet. He had articles that were published; he ghostwrote a few columns, but he'd used up every cent of his savings for this flight from JFK to Miami International and the connection to Marsh Harbor. Still, he had enough dollars in his wallet for coffee and that was a positive thing. With his second cup in his hand, he glanced up at the board. Somehow he'd killed time looking at pictures of paradise and thinking about how badly the meeting with Connor had gone, and now the board showed the gate was open.

He wasn't in any hurry, and he didn't have the need to be first in any queue. So he joined pretty much at the end, listening to people talking, seeing the heads of first class as they were allowed on before what he liked to call 'cattle class'. When he made his way to the front, they checked his boarding pass and he followed the crowd into the plane. He always found it so funny the rest of the passengers had to walk through first to get to their places at the back of the aircraft. First-class passengers, business men, a couple of kids, all checking out the goodies around their reclining seats. Shaun stepped aside to let a hostess pass and bumped back into one of these first-class passengers. Turning a little to apologize, he came face-to-face with Connor *freaking* French.

They stared at each other long enough to be uncomfortable, short enough that they didn't have to talk, then Shaun was swept along by the hostess and a couple of last minute stragglers getting on the plane. Only when in his seat, with the curtain pulled between first class and the rest did it sink in why Connor was on this plane.

It could just be coincidence, but…

Was Connor going to Sapphire Cay as well?

He didn't see Connor when they landed at Miami. First class was empty, all the passengers in that rarefied air having disembarked first. He'd spent the entire flight from JFK thinking about what he would say to Connor when they saw each other, he was kind of happy not to have to talk to him.

Connor probably had business in Miami. Just because he was heading to Florida didn't mean that he was going to the Cay. Why would he be? The way he shut Shaun and the questioning down was evidence to suggest Connor wasn't doing anything more than toeing the party line from the French family.

The humidity hit him like a punch to the face as he pushed through the airport doors and got his first taste of Florida in June. The flight landed early afternoon and the air was oppressive. This was why he'd spent the last few years in London, no sticky, sweaty weather and certainly no sky-crushing thunderstorms which threatened now.

I'm following a story, he told himself. *A remarkable story.* One his publisher was excited about, one that Shaun's dad was excited about, ever since they'd found the box in the attic after Shaun's grandfather had died. James Jamieson, or JJ to his friends had passed away at Christmas and the grief of losing a grandparent was still high in Shaun. JJ hadn't exactly spoken much about his father Alfie, not much beyond the fact he'd fought in the Pacific in World War II, and that he'd died of cancer back in the sixties.

No one had known he'd been in love with someone else before marrying. His marriage wasn't big enough to hit the society pages, nor was the birth of his son, JJ. No one had known the person he'd been in love with before had been a man. Peter French. And the letters were haunting and emotional and Shaun cried when he first read them. The norms of society had kept Peter and Alfie apart, but Shaun wanted to tell their story. A story that was seventy years old and one the French Foundation was closing down at every turn.

When he had his fill of the sticky air, he went back inside. He now had a fifty-five minute connecting flight to Marsh Harbor in the Bahamas and he doubted the pond jumper was going to be like the passenger airline he'd flown in on.

Suitably fuelled with enough coffee to float a boat and a burger that cost more than he'd wanted to spend, he climbed on the small plane. He sighed to himself when he realized that this short flight was going to happen with him in a tiny seat all hunched up. At times like this, being six foot tall was a drawback. He maneuvered past the flight attendant who shot him a blinding white grin as she checked his boarding card. There was no first class, there was no separation. This was a utilitarian flight and yes, his worst fears were quickly confirmed. Two rows from the cockpit, looking like someone had pissed in his breakfast, sat Connor French.

They saw each other at the same time and Connor's

expression was a comical parody of exasperation and shock. He stood up, hitting his head on the overhead bin but not even acknowledging it.

"What are you doing here?" he asked.

Shaun hoisted his flight bag higher and glanced down at his ticket; thank God he was a couple rows behind Connor, who was now actually rubbing at the point on his head he'd hit. *He feels pain, he's not made of stone.*

How should he handle this one? Remote politeness? Indifference? Connor said something and every idea of being rational were slammed.

"I'll get a restraining order," Connor said firmly. The woman sitting beside him, in the aisle, shrunk back in her seat. She was fanning herself with the flight safety card and looked from Connor to Shaun with both interest and concern.

"Restraining me from what?" Shaun asked evenly. He'd heard crap like this before. "Freedom of speech?"

Connor's expression blanked; his lips tight. He was a gorgeous guy, but there was way too much control in the way he stood. Too much stress in the frown on his face, lines bracketing his eyes, evidence that he never allowed himself to relax.

"From harassing my family."

Shaun opened his mouth to speak, but the steward coughed to intervene. "Sir, could you take your seat, please?"

Shaun did as he was told, pushing his flight bag into the storage and shutting the door. He could see the top of Connor's head from where he stood but as soon as he sat it was like he wasn't on the same plane as Connor.

The journey was slow, in the wispy clouds, the storm behind them in Miami, and by the time they reached Marsh Harbor, Shaun was ready to get off the damn bone-rattling plane.

Connor was there first, pushing past the woman sitting next to him who was struggling to get her bag down. Shaun helped her and she thanked him with a smile and a roll of her eyes thrown at Connor's retreating back.

"Your boyfriend is pissed," she said.

"Yeah," Shaun answered. So sue him if he couldn't be bothered to correct her. He had words to say to Connor and phone calls to make. His dad had warned him this might happen, the rich, old, established family would try and close Shaun down. He hadn't believed him; no one protected secrets that old now, surely. His dad called him naive, in that affectionate way only a parent could do.

As soon as he was off the plane he found a signal and connected to his dad, but there was no reply, so he left a long rambling message. "The French Foundation has sent someone down to the Cay," he began. "Connor, a suit-wearing great-nephew with a stick up his preppy fucking ass, wants to shut this down. I'm ignoring him, but he's threatening lawyers. Can you ask Emma if he has any grounds for that, and call me back? Meanwhile, I'm still going to the island." Emma, his cousin, was a lawyer, and she'd warned Shaun that things could get tricky. But Shaun wasn't born yesterday; his artistic integrity was sound. He took his responsibilities as a journalist seriously. He knew what he could and couldn't write, and he'd be willing to go to court to fight it.

He ended the call and turned to find screens showing

where his luggage would appear. Marsh Harbor wasn't very big and it turned out his luggage was as easy to spot as Connor. He too was on the phone and his posture shouted angry, defeated, then angry again. Shaun noticed people walking around him, giving him a wide berth, but somehow, he was pulled in closer.

"…and it's not like I can stop him…it's just a story. Gramps…that's ridiculous…okay…" A big sigh, then Connor ended the call. For a second he too looked around him, clearly checking for baggage claim. He turned enough to see Shaun standing next to him and the anger fled, in its place was a cold politeness.

Shaun decided to offer an olive branch. "Seems we're going to the same place then."

Connor narrowed his eyes, and Shaun couldn't help but notice the tension in Connor's face, or the whiteness of his knuckles as he gripped his cell.

"You could go back," Connor said. Someone knocked into Shaun and he half turned to apologize and to move aside. They were standing barriers to everyone around them.

"I'm going to the Cay."

"Even if you destroy innocent lives?" Fire lit in Connor's eyes.

Shaun shook his head. "Jesus, that's a bit dramatic don't you think?"

Connor stepped closer, near enough so that Shaun could smell the deodorant Connor used, or maybe cologne. Whatever it turned out to be, it was fresh and he inhaled.

"How much money would it take?" Connor asked.

"My grandfather has agreed to a financial remuneration should you back off."

Shaun sighed inwardly. He'd been expecting this for a long time. Money wasn't something he'd been looking for. Even if he had been the kind of unprincipled man who could be bought off, how could he betray this need inside him to put his family's history to paper? How could he begin to tell a man who had the money to keep secrets safe that this wasn't actually a stealthy mistake that should stay closed in a box? The love story was beautiful and it should be made real.

"Nothing," Shaun said. "I promise you couldn't pay me anything."

"Every man has his price point," Connor said, firm and to the point.

Shaun fought the sudden desire to take a step back and away from Connor, who seemed to be attempting to intimidate physically and verbally. "I'm not every man. I don't know who you do business with but not everyone can be bought," he said.

Connor leaned closer. "They won't let this go." With that he turned on his heel, grabbed a case and with his flight bag on his shoulder, he stalked away. Shaun took a little more time to get his stuff; he didn't really want to be walking with gorgeous-but-overbearing, and frankly-scary-idiot Connor. *They won't let this go*, was a very telling statement. Connor admitting something like that implied it was possible Connor was doing what he was told. Perhaps Connor could be reasoned with? Still, the way Connor was striding away gave all kinds of 'keep away from me' messages.

Only when Shaun made it outside into the hot but not quite so oppressive air did he realize how fucked both of them were. The only way to the Cay was by boat, but maybe there would be two trips and he could go over alone? Then he saw the sign and his stomach sank. Jamieson/French. No peace then. They were going to be on the same boat.

Maybe I can get Connor to talk?

The man holding the sign had been kissed by the sun. He had tanned skin, light brown hair, and looked more like a surfer than a staff member. He was already talking to Connor, as he held the sign high.

"...you're both our guests," the man was saying. He sounded confused and given what Connor had likely laid on him the poor man probably didn't know what to think.

Connor replied, but he was talking low and had his back to Shaun.

"I'm Jamieson, Shaun Jamieson," Shaun interrupted, and maneuvered around Connor, with his hand outstretched, which tall surfer guy shook firmly.

"Hello, Shaun, I'm Dylan Gray. Nice to put a face to the phone calls and emails."

"Sure is."

"Welcome to the Bahamas."

The three men stood awkwardly. Connor taut and fuming, Dylan's smile of welcome turning to a quirk of puzzlement, Shaun trying not to let his temper push over his more agreeable side.

Dylan coughed. "So, let's go then."

He turned smartly on his heel and both Shaun and Connor followed until they came to the harbor itself, a bustling hive of activity, people buying and selling, tourists with cameras. They didn't talk to each other but Shaun enjoyed the view as he trailed both Dylan and Connor. The view of Connor in particular, with his suit pants and the tucked-in pristine white shirt which didn't look wrinkled despite the plane journeys here.

It's a shame the guy is such an asshole.

"This is the Lady Liberty," Dylan announced with pride in his voice. He jumped down to the worn-looking boat with practiced ease then reached up a hand. "Pass down your luggage," he instructed. Connor did so, Shaun next, then Connor began the short climb down to the flat boat. Shaun waited until Connor was standing steadily in the vessel before taking the steps down. When finally they were onboard, Dylan indicated where Shaun should sit and he didn't argue. That he had to sit next to Connor wasn't important. He was safe on the boat, and he put on the lifejacket when it was handed to him. No one need know he couldn't really swim and that he had an abject fear of water he couldn't see the bottom of. Nope, that was something he wasn't going to share.

"Ready?" Dylan asked. Connor nodded, as did Shaun, and with a slightly jerky motion the Liberty moved from the harbor and out into the smooth blue water. They sat in silence until Dylan decided conversation had to be had.

"So," he began. "What was the journey like?"

"Good," Connor said.

"Hot but good," Shaun said at the same time.

And that was the conversation all done. Until inspiration hit Shaun. Forget talking directly to Connor until they were on the island and alone, forget the fact he had Connor sitting next to him and that every so often they would bump arms. Ignore the simmering tension between them.

"So how was your and Lucas's wedding?" he asked. Connor flashed him a quick look and Shaun felt like he'd scored points in some kind of game of one-upmanship. *Take that closet man, gay people get married, so suck it up.*

"A wonderful day," Dylan said. He was smiling, Shaun could hear it in his voice, but evidently Dylan couldn't take his hands off the wheel or his eyes off the flat shimmering horizon. Sweat trickled down Shaun's back and for a second running his hands in the cool water seemed like a good thing. "Seems more special by the day considering the history of this place."

"Yeah. Like the whole Peter/Alfie story came full circle with you and your husband on the island," Shaun said. Shaun knew he was deliberately poking the hornet's nest.

Silence. Connor said nothing. He didn't look at Shaun, and pretty much that was how the entire journey to Sapphire Cay was. Awkward sentences exchanged between him and an increasingly wary Dylan with Connor not saying a word. Every so often Liberty's engine would hitch and the boat would shudder, and each time Shaun's stomach fell and he gripped the life jacket hard.

Sapphire Cay became more than a smudge on the horizon, the shape of it defined. The palm trees reached for the blue sky and the house finally came into view. Shaun felt excitement grip him. He wondered what his great-great granddad thought when he first saw this island. Was he excited, scared, or had love made everything perfect?

For a second, he imagined Peter waiting on the jetty, Alfie jumping from the boat and them falling into each other's arms. Of course, it probably hadn't happened that way. Back then you couldn't hug and love in public if you were two men, but Shaun could see the love in his imagination. Next to him Connor shifted in his seat.

"Mr. Gray, I'll need a meeting as soon as we land," he announced with the boat maybe twenty feet from the jetty. "Once everything is signed, I'll need to get back to Marsh Harbor."

"Tomorrow morning, and call me Dylan," Dylan said. His tone brooked no discussion and even though Connor cursed under his breath he didn't push the issue.

Dylan slowed the engine, allowing Liberty to smoothly float to the jetty. Shaun stood up as soon as the boat came to a halt next to the wooden dock. He made it look like it was less about getting off the boat and more about helping out tall, dark and gorgeous who was tying off the boat. This would be Scott, he recalled from the photos of the island and its staff. He waited for Connor and Dylan, but Dylan stopped Connor as he made to get off the boat and said something low and soft.

What he said Shaun couldn't hear, but it was enough to have Connor bristle with a temper which Dylan ignored. Connor scrambled up off the boat and pushed past Shaun, then with his feet sinking in the sand he walked up the beach dragging his case behind him as best as he could.

"What happened there?" Scott asked.

Dylan shook his head and pointedly looked at Shaun.

"Don't ask. Scott, can you take a look at Liberty? She doesn't sound good."

"Will do."

Then Dylan turned to him, "We gonna have any problems with you and Connor?" he asked, steel-eyed and focused.

Shaun had a whole speech about how he was here for good reasons, how Connor was being a dick, how Shaun was going to persuade Connor and the rest of the French family to support this project. Instead, it didn't seem appropriate to say a thing about what he wanted. Dylan and Lucas had extended an invite to Shaun as a guest, and Shaun was a proper Seattle kid, all polite and thoughtful. "No. No problem I can't handle."

Dylan nodded. "There're no other guests, and we only got the call Connor was visiting a couple of days ago."

Connor must have been straight on the phone making the call and booking flights the second Shaun had left his office.

"I didn't feel right saying no to him when we'd already said yes to you. Those letters are part of both your families' histories, so I'd like to think this can be civil. But if you're going to kill each other, can you make sure it's near the water so we don't have far to drag the bodies?" Dylan smiled, but there was intent in his words. To hide bodies maybe not, but Dylan was going to lose respect for Shaun if all he and Connor did was fight.

"There will be no killing," Shaun said.

Dylan looked up at the retreating Connor. "He's not here to talk is he?"

Shaun shook his head no. "He's on the island to shut this whole story down."

"Then I guess you're a lucky guy."

"In what way?"

Dylan handed over one of the bags from the boat to Scott. "He was supposed to come here at the end of February. But he didn't because of clashes with our bookings and his diary. Honestly, I thought the French Foundation decided the letters we had weren't worth their time. But then you got in touch and it was like maybe we'd finally found someone to take Peter and Alfie home."

"But then the French family contacted you again." Going to see Connor at his office had alerted him to the fact there was somebody else out there who knew the truth. They had feared the secret love affair might not stay secret. Shaun cursed his stupidity. He should have come out to Sapphire Cay first, then approached Connor with both sets of letters.

"I hope you can come to some agreement."

Me too.

"I wish Lucas were here," Dylan muttered. Then he hefted the largest case, Shaun's, which Shaun took from him. "Let's get up to the house."

Chapter Seven

DYLAN GAVE SCOTT THE LOOK, THE ONE THAT SAID, 'please for fuck's sake take over'. The vibes he'd felt in the crossing to the Cay weren't good ones, and the idea of getting in the middle of a heated debate wasn't on his to-do list. He had enough to worry about without adding two warring men and an old feud. He locked the office door and considered what had happened – exactly what Lucas had warned him would happen. He wanted to phone Lucas, but the baby coming early was enough family stress without Dylan dumping loads of shit on his husband. Lucas would be back in a few days, all being well, then Dylan would be able to clear his head. Right now there was only one other person he could talk to.

He placed the call before he could second guess himself and phoned the only person who would listen to him right at this moment.

"Mitch Stone."

Mitch's tone was reassuringly very similar to the one

Lucas used to such good effect, all calm and confident and Dylan relaxed marginally.

"I fucked up," Dylan announced. Then he heard some movement rustling, a door closing, and Mitch's voice sounding different like he was in a cupboard.

"I'm in a meeting," Mitch said. "This had better be good."

Weirdly enough, after the wedding, Dylan and Mitch had grown to be friends again, both loved up and acknowledging they were exactly wrong for each other.

"You know the Alfie/Peter thing."

"The guys on the island from the War? I remember."

"Look, do you have five minutes?"

Mitch sighed. Then he chuckled. "They won't miss me for a bit. Jeez, if Isaac could see me sitting in a damn supply closet he'd never let me live it down. Go on, you have five."

"Ok, well, you remember Connor French?"

"No."

"He's the guy who was supposed to be visiting before the wedding but it never happened. Well he's here."

"I'm not following."

"He's the great-great something to the original Peter French and he's here. But there's another someone here, who got in touch the middle of last month."

"Wait, before you go on...I need to ask you, how is Tash? Her baby girl?"

"She's well. They both are."

"We sent flowers and a pink teddy for Francesca. That was what they named her, right? But that's beside the point, carry on with the story. It's riveting."

"Are you yanking my chain?"

"A bit. But go on anyway. I get I am a surrogate Lucas in having to listen to this latest drama."

"Asshole. This guy, Shaun Jamieson, is here as well. And he's the great-great something grandson of Alfie Jamieson. The AJ we knew was Alfie is actually Alfie Jamieson. Are you following this?"

Mitch went quiet for a moment, then summarized. "You have the great-great somethings of the original Alfie/Peter on the Cay. I'm following."

"Yeah well, Shaun has this bundle of letters and he wanted to come to the island and visit and see what we had to work out a proper history. He's writing a book."

"Okay," There was some noise of shuffling and a curse before a loud clatter. "Fucking hell, that's bleach…" then another curse and some more clattering. "You owe me one for this, Gray."

"I feel like I should apologize."

"I'll send you the dry-cleaning bill. So, this all sounds like a good thing, both descendants on the island, you could make a movie from that."

"Lucas told me after Connor French got in touch that I should have told them that they'd both be here, but I didn't listen," Dylan blurted. "And I couldn't go back to Shaun and say we'd changed our minds. Or say no to Connor, because it turned out he'd already booked flights."

Silence. Another sigh. "Lucas gave you advice that you chose to ignore?" Unspoken was *you freaking idiot* on the end.

Dylan immediately felt defensive despite knowing the comment was valid. "Shaun wants to write a book. This great World War II love story about forbidden love, honoring his ancestor and so on. He's a journalist and he sent me some of what he'd done and it's good."

"But."

"Connor French, on the other hand, wants us to sign a non-disclosure agreement and give up everything to the French Foundation. He doesn't want the story out there."

"So...um...why are they on the island at the same time?"

"Because I thought it would be a good idea," Dylan said miserably.

More silence and Dylan could swear he heard Mitch trying not to laugh. "But Lucas disagreed."

"He said we should have them here one at a time and see both sides. He doesn't agree the story should be forgotten, but he says it's not our place to comment."

"Dylan, what is it you want me to say exactly?"

Dylan kicked up his feet and placed them on the table, leaning back in his chair. Lucas would kill him if he saw him, Dylan with his size tens up on Lucas's beloved work area, but while the cat was away... "I don't know. I'm just avoiding being out there with the warring sides."

"They're fighting. Jesus, Dylan, you should have listened to Lucas. Is that what you wanted me to say?"

Dylan ignored the fact that this was probably exactly what he should hear. "They're not fighting, well not physically. Shaun is all *I love this island* and questions, while Connor is all, *we need a meeting to close this story down*. They are clearly at an impasse."

"So, sort it." Mitch offered. Another clatter, another curse.

"Sort it how?"

"Shut them in a room and lock the door, and Dylan, for God's sake, stay out of it."

Dylan nodded then realized Mitch wouldn't be able to see him. "Okay. Tomorrow, I'll do it tomorrow."

"When is Lucas coming home?"

Dylan didn't have to think of the answer. "Four days, three hours."

"Good, now can I go? I think this fucking bucket really had bleach in it."

"Sorry," Dylan offered. "But tie-dye is fashionable you know. Ask Isaac."

"Fuck you, Dylan." Mitch chuckled along with the words that held no heat.

"And you, Mitchell."

Mitch rang off and Dylan was left with a dead connection. Carefully, he replaced the handset and leaned back in the seat, startled when there was a knock on the door.

Oh God, they found me.

"Dylan, let me in," Scott called from outside.

Dylan stood up and brushed the desk where there was sand deposited. Sand was a hazard of living on an island, but it wouldn't be good for Lucas to find it under his penholder when he came home. Then he'd know Dylan had put his feet on the desk.

He let Scott in, who had a frown on his face and oil in a long streak from temple to chin on the left-hand side.

"You left me with them," he began, "but that isn't the worst of it."

"Shit, what did they do?"

"Nothing," Scott said with a shake of his head. "Connor is in fourteen and Shaun is in three and Adam has made dinner. There was a bit of sarcasm from the journalist, Shaun, but that Connor guy is one cold dude. He tipped me ten dollars though."

"So if they're not causing trouble, what is?"

Scott sighed and his shoulders dropped. "Liberty, she's not doing so well."

Liberty was Scott's responsibility now, well, his and Dylan's. Although Lucas had talked them around about getting a new boat, one he would be bringing back himself in four days, Liberty was Dylan's first boat and his baby. "She didn't sound right on the way over."

"We need to order in parts, but she's stuck where she is until we get them."

Dylan nodded. "We can take her back to Marsh Harbor tomorrow for parts."

Scott shook his head. "I'm not feeling that, Dylan. She's shaky and I think we should do the work here."

"She won't make it back to Marsh Harbor?"

"Yeah, maybe, probably, hell, I don't want to chance it."

Dylan thought on his feet. "Okay, email the details to Lucas, ask him to grab what we need and bring it back on Liberty Two when he's picked her up."

Scott rubbed his hands with a towel as he spoke. The towel was as oily as his skin. "We need a better name than Liberty Two," he mused.

"Yeah, yeah," Dylan said. He liked the name, however impractical it was.

After three more months of searching and of Lucas giving Dylan pointed looks after multiple trips to Marsh Harbor with guests, they had eventually found a new boat Dylan deemed worthy to join the family. Better late than never, he had tried to convince Lucas when Lucas shared his not so subtle observation that the season was over and they then had more boats than guests.

He pursed his lips. If only they had been able to pick it up sooner. He and Scott could have collected Shaun and Connor separately.

"And you're okay with Lucas bringing the new boat back?"

Dylan nodded. "He knows what to do; he'll be fine."

Scott turned to leave then turned just outside the door. "Adam said dinner at seven out by the pool."

Dylan stretched tall. He wasn't looking forward to dinner with Shaun and Connor, but he was the host and he needed to prevent them from killing each other. Either that or sit back and start selling tickets to the fight of the century.

I should have listened to Lucas.

———

CONNOR ANSWERED THE CALL AFTER THREE RINGS. HE'D put his phone on charge and he had to scramble to get it to his ear, but at least it snapped him out of broodily staring out the window. All he could see was sea, sky, and beach, and all he wanted was to be down on that beach, by the sea, staring up at the endless blue.

He grimaced when he saw who it was. Annalisa never called unless she had to. She preferred meeting up for quiet lunches in sophisticated surroundings than talking on the phone.

"Aunt Annalisa," he answered formally.

"Connor, darling," she began grandly. She always did things splendidly but in perfect taste. With her pearls and her Chanel suits, she was a society leader, the visual reminder of who the New York Bainbridges were, and the influence they still wielded in business. She may well have divorced Peter French in 1942, but she was also still very much part of the French Foundation, organizing fundraising events all the way up until last year when she'd suffered a mini-stroke.

Now she was quieter, but she was still in control and Connor loved her for it.

"Is everything okay?" Connor asked when Annalisa didn't immediately launch into some explanation of why she needed something done and would Connor be a pet and do it for her. She didn't know he was on Sapphire Cay, so he'd need to think on his feet.

"So, I know you're on Sapphire Cay," she began.

Ahh, so there went the need to pretend. "You do?"

"Yes, yes, Connor dear; I want you to do something for me."

"I'm shutting it down like you asked," Connor interjected swiftly. He expected praise, but all he got was a loud tut.

"I never said such a thing." She sounded horrified. "Your grandfather seems to think Peter's story should be hidden, but I have no issues with the story being written.

Oscar called me yesterday in a panic; seems he was worried you wouldn't be able to do the job you'd been sent to do; something about you being not entirely unbiased in the situation."

At first that made no sense, but just as quickly Connor put two and two together. The *gay* thing, it had to be. *Jesus*, Connor muttered under his breath. Oscar French had outwardly accepted Connor was gay. He'd said that a grandfather should always love their grandson and just want them happy. He'd been openly supportive, but at the end of the day, Oscar French was the old guard. Apparently, being the nephew of a gay man in the forties had made him bitter and had left him harboring issues he didn't show to the public or to Connor. He just hinted at them every so often. Connor knew that his grandfather was disappointed in him, which is why he kept his private life just that, private. Oscar probably thought Connor would be swayed by the story.

"Hello? Are you there, Connor?"

"Sorry, I am."

"Seems to me," his aunt continued with great confidence in her voice, "after all these years, the stories should at least be made whole."

"Really?" Connor wasn't convinced. He'd been listening to his granddad for so long that he had probably let himself be talked out of any opposing opinion.

"Oh, Connor," she said on a sigh. "I for one would love to know about the man who had my husband's heart. And not in a bad way. I loved Peter. When you get to my age, you have an awful lot of time for navel gazing, Connor." She was wistful and went quiet for a little while, then in a smaller voice she added, "I would only have wanted him to be happy."

"You're sure?" Connor didn't mean to sound like he doubted his aunt. But wasn't she worried about what people would think? After all, opinion meant a lot to Annalisa.

"I want you to…" her voice trailed off and Connor wondered if the line had dropped, but a quick look at the screen saw them still connected. Seemed she was just considering what to say, which was strange in itself. Annalisa Bainbridge never actually paused with what she wanted to say and this was the second time in the same conversation. "I didn't love Peter. Not as much as I wanted to, not as much as I needed to. I know you hear it all the time, but things were different then. The marriage wasn't arranged as such, but it was expected. The Bainbridges connecting with the French family."

"I understand that."

"I'd like to know that…"

"What?" Connor prompted after another pause.

"We never talked about it, about the needs he had outside of…we didn't ever speak of the man he loved… I need to know that he found happiness somehow. Find that for me, Connor?"

Connor nodded. "I can try."

"Good, good." The uncertainty in Annalisa's voice was replaced by a brisk purpose. "We will converse anon." Then she ended the call and Connor was staring at a blank charging phone.

That was a change around. Connor had been sent here by Peter's nephew to close this story down, and now he had been tasked by Peter's ex-wife with finding out if Peter had been happy.

"Screwed," he muttered to the empty room.

He exited the room, closing and locking the door behind him before taking the stairs down to the ground floor. He stopped to look at the view from the window. The stretch of beach beyond the palm trees was sparkling in the lower evening sun and he bet the sea was warm. There was a pool. He'd spotted it on the way in and his swimmer's soul ached to be out in the water somehow. Maybe after he managed to pin Dylan down to talk tonight, though Dylan had suggested tomorrow, he could get up super early and maybe have some time in the pool. He couldn't actually remember the last time he'd had a swim outside under a blue sky. The pool in his apartment building was small and had been built in the basement. Not even using huge gilt mirrors to give the illusion of space had helped.

But Sapphire Cay? There was no doubting this place was beautiful. He could see why someone would want to stay here for a vacation.

Just not me. I don't have time for vacations.

He had too many things to look after. The Foundation, the family legacy, and that was just the start of the list.

Dylan had disappeared as soon as they set foot on the jetty, but he'd be at dinner and that was as good as a formal meeting. Connor knew most things got done in more informal surroundings. His grandfather's words rang in his ears, *don't let this hurt Annalisa.* Then Annalisa herself, *I need to know he found happiness.* Talk about a rock and a hard place.

He was down at dinner with a half hour to spare, so he headed to the beach. As soon as he reached the sand he removed his socks and shoes. This place reminded him of childhood summers in Martha's Vineyard with his parents and the feel of the sand was enough to have him standing absolutely still and closing his eyes for a second. So many memories flooded him, of a time when all he had was the water and the sand and the promise of endless days laid out in front of him.

He moved only when the lure of hunger had him moving closer to the hotel. There was a large table set for five, water glasses, cutlery. The view from all sides, house or sea, was stunning. He placed his shoes on the chair with the view of the water, kind of saving it for himself, and went over to the pool. Not particularly big, it was still enough to get a decent workout and he was lured by the cool sparkling blue to sit on the edge and dangle his feet in the water.

"We need to talk," a voice came from behind, and all the water in the world couldn't stop him tensing. He turned to look back at Shaun, who was standing by the table with a large notebook in hand.

"No. We don't," Connor said. "I need to call a formal meeting with Dylan so I can put this to bed." *So I can get my head around who wants what from whom.*

Shaun said nothing for a little while, nor did he come closer. He placed the book very deliberately on the chair next to the one Connor had reserved with his shoes, and spoke. "I don't understand why you don't want to talk. Why are you here if you don't want this resolved after knowing all the facts?"

Connor turned back to look at the pool. "This will be fixed," he said. "Dylan will sign over everything to the Foundation, and our lawyers have prepared an airtight legal document allowing no information of what allegedly happened to leave this island." Somewhere in there would be information that he could give to Annalisa, and he would also fulfill his obligations to his grandfather. This could well be win/win.

"What about the letters and notes that I have?" Shaun said with no small amount of sarcasm in his voice. "You going to shut me down too?"

Connor stiffened. No one had told him that someone else had any evidence to support the stories. As far as he was aware it was only the letters the Sapphire Cay owners had found on the island. He swung his feet from the water and in a smooth move he stood, the material of his pants snagging on his wet ankles.

Shaun looked really confused but utterly immovable. He wasn't lying, or trying to encourage Connor to do anything stupid. He had more information, that was truth somehow, and getting that information for Annalisa made Connor's job all that more difficult.

"What are you talking about?" Connor asked.

"When my grandfather died, we found a whole pile of letters and a journal, and proof that Alfie and Peter met again in 1966, the year Alfie died."

Well, that would be Annalisa's happy ever after, he thought. "I need to take those letters too."

Shaun pointed at the folder. "I have copies here for you to read. Feel free to have a look. The originals are in a safe place."

Connor considered scooping the copies up and throwing them into the sea. Not that this would end whatever shit Shaun could cause to Connor's family if they were only copies.

Connor could say to Annalisa that Peter and Alfie met up and that they resolved things. But that would leave Shaun still out there with information that could potentially hurt the French Foundation. He had images of throwing Shaun in the sea as well, and he pushed the thoughts aside. This was a situation to be handled and water wasn't going to solve this one.

"Letters that prove nothing," he said.

Shaun tilted his head a little. "You're right. Until I match them to the things that they found here, I won't know for sure. But I've seen photocopies of what Dylan and Lucas have here and I'm convinced this island was another chapter in my great-great-grandfather's life. The final chapter. I've started the book and I want the whole story, not just half of it."

Connor pushed back the exasperation he felt. "You don't know how many people you will hurt if you insist on doing this."

"Who?" Shaun looked confused. "Who would I hurt? Peter and Alfie are both dead, being gay is more accepted now in the mainstream, and it's a beautiful love story."

"Not everyone in this story you want to tell is dead," Connor said.

"Annalisa? I want to talk to her, get her side." Shaun took a couple steps toward him, his hands out in entreaty. "Just get her to talk to me. Your grandfather shut me down, but if I could get to Annalisa herself."

An hour ago Connor would have said there was no point approaching Annalisa for anything, not if she'd already told Shaun she wouldn't talk, but what if she hadn't? What if this was all on his granddad? The old man causing issues? What if Shaun meeting Annalisa was the only way around all of this? Shaun meets Annalisa, sees the person he could be hurting, and he doesn't write the book.

"Is everything okay?" a voice came from behind them and they both spun to see a man carrying dishes. This had to be Adam, the final person on the island, chef, golden brown eyes, slim, spiky hair, sexy. Scott walked up beside Adam with a tray of cocktails and a smile.

"They're fine," Scott said with determination. "Ignore them."

Connor raised an eyebrow. Should the staff be talking about them that way? Then he glanced at Shaun and realized what they must look like; a couple of idiot kids. They'd moved closer into a classic face-off position, each bristling with a kind of righteous indignation. Deliberately he stepped back to break the deadlock.

"My apologies," he said softly. He turned to the table, moved his shoes, and took his seat. He needed to change his game plan. Annalisa wanted to know if there had been a happy ever after, while Oscar wanted the story buried. Connor could do both. Starting with using some of the French charm that he'd inherited from his father. Shaun seemed like a nice guy, and Connor should treat this like he would meeting any new person. First off, he would stop acting out as a result of the dire warnings that his grandfather had given him. He should listen to his heart and get to know every side of this before judging. All he had to do was remember that he loved Annalisa and he wanted to protect her.

I am my own man.

"So, Shaun, how long have you been writing?"

Chapter Eight

SHAUN CLOSED THE DOOR TO HIS ROOM, THE QUANTITY OF bright green cocktails he'd consumed messing with his equilibrium. He made it to the bed and sprawled onto the white covers. Didn't matter that he had drunk enough cocktails to take the edge off, he was still way past irritated with Connor *freaking confusing* French and he needed ten minutes to get his head straight.

The man had only stayed for food then excused himself with a headache. A *headache, for fuck's sake*. Anyone with half a brain saw it for what the excuse was and that was avoidance. They'd chatted sensibly for a while; Shaun about his writing and Connor about whatever it was he did for the French Foundation. Adam and Scott, along with Dylan, talked and kept the conversation going. Of course, Scott supplied the cocktails which tasted just like a drink on a tropical island should; ever so slightly *coconutty* and a whole lot *rummish*. Coconutty and rummish were *definitely* words.

Sighing, he flopped over on his back and lay spread-eagled under the lazily moving ceiling fan. He knew it was his fault Connor had disappeared. In fact, he'd known the very second he'd crossed the line with the other man, who to be fair was sitting and talking in a very civilized fashion. The question had been bubbling away inside Shaun since he'd first met Connor. If anything, it had been there longer than that. But yeah, vocalizing his question had caused Connor's eyes to narrow and his affable I'll-talk-to-anyone expression to be replaced with anger.

Clearly your heart is dead if you don't believe in love.

"I should have kept my mouth shut," he said to the empty room. The words mocked him. *Yes, you should have*, his conscience replied. Connor hadn't said he didn't believe in love, just that there was no need to pull up Alfie and Peter's love. Shaun was on edge about this whole thing; the project was his baby, and Alfie was his family.

The knock on the door was loud and sudden and startled the shit out of Shaun. He sat bolt upright in his bed and wished he hadn't when the room spun. What the hell?

"Hey? Are you back yet?"

Shaun groaned. Connor was at his door. Connor with his come-to-bed brown eyes, and his tight ass, and his thighs all solid and his lips that kissable side of plump. Outside Shaun's damn door.

"What do you want?" Shaun asked. At least Connor's knocking and the subsequent shock cleared his head a little.

"Shaun?"

"Connor, go away."

"I want to talk."

"It's midnight."

"This can't wait."

"Yes, it can."

"No, it can't."

Jesus.

Shaun swung his legs and pushed to stand. Clearly Connor wasn't listening to him shouting through the door, so face-to-face it had to be. Squaring his shoulders, he crossed to the door, which was no more than a few steps away, and threw it open with a flourish.

"What?" he asked. He was aiming for a tone of exasperation, but the sight of Connor standing on his threshold looking disheveled and tired was enough for the 'what' to come out soft and tired.

"Can I come in?" Connor's soft voice matched the slump in his body.

Shaun glanced behind him. He hadn't even unpacked yet, and the room was too small to chance having Connor in here with him. Connor messed with his head in open spaces, let alone in this room.

"No," Shaun said. Connor frowned. "I need some air," Shaun qualified. Connor's frown disappeared and he again had that hopeful expression on his face. "Let's go for a walk." Shaun pocketed his key and closed the door behind him, realizing at the last moment that Connor hadn't actually moved and they were now quite close.

Close enough for Shaun to reach and touch Connor if he wanted. He didn't. In a step that could have been smooth if he weren't a little drunk, and which looked more like a duck and weave, he was passing Connor. They headed outside and used the small set of stairs that went down to the sands at the back of the hotel. Shaun removed his shoes and placed them on the bottom step and Connor followed suit. Silently they walked away from the hotel and to the beach. This side of the hotel had the same soft lighting as the pool and the jetty but had been left wilder, the plants and stones a vibrant tumble down to the ocean. By silent agreement, they walked until they were inches from the lapping waves. Then they stopped.

"What you said," Connor began.

"I'm sorry," Shaun interjected before Connor could call him on his idiocy.

"It's true though, not all of it, I mean, I'm capable of falling in love." Connor stopped and tilted his head up look at the stars. "I think I am. Can't say I've been in love before." He looked back at Shaun. "But I know it's out there, and one day I'll find my very own Alfie and everything will be good."

Shaun was blown away. He blamed the cocktails, made a curious and embarrassing groan sound, and subsided to sit cross-legged on the sand.

Connor followed his lead. "Are you drunk?" he asked, curious and with laughter in his voice. Or was Shaun imagining the laughter?

"Adam took my last drink and added this thing, as well as Scott's thing, then Dylan did…"

"A thing."

"Yeah. And it tasted nice, but I think…the thing…" Shaun shook his head to clear his thoughts. Luckily the alcohol was enough to take the edge off the embarrassment at this weird situation he was in.

"The thing, yeah…" Connor shifted on the sand a little and they knocked knees. He apologized softly and scooted back a little. "Anyway, I called Annalisa, and my grandfather when I was back in the room. I was angry…"

"With them?"

"With you."

"Oh."

"So, I'm going to lay this on the table, get everything out there. Is that okay?"

Shaun nodded. The alcohol edge to his thoughts was diminishing, probably a mix of listening to Connor, being *attracted* to Connor, and the fact that it was a little chilly down here by the water. Nothing like Seattle cold, but way colder than the burning tropical sun of earlier.

"Go for it," he encouraged when Connor didn't immediately begin.

"My grandfather is real old school, and he remembers the scandals from a kid's perspective. Things whispered about my great-great-uncle, about Peter, that he wasn't normal, and that it was all too much for the family to bear. You have to remember my grandfather is in his seventies and he was born into a very different world, added to which he tells me I have the Foundation's reputation to protect."

Shaun couldn't see where this was going. So he said nothing about anything, he just listened.

"He says that secrets should stay buried, that the shame Peter brought to the family as a gay man is the same as he feels when he looks at me sometimes, blah blah blah." Connor made a motion with his fingers like a quacking duck then rolled his eyes which Shaun could see in the moonlight. "Nothing I hadn't heard before, not since I came out when I was nineteen. I don't have any siblings, neither did my dad, so when he died…" Connor paused for a moment, lost in his thoughts. Then he continued with a stronger voice. "When my dad died, it all happened when I was at college and my grandfather was there for me. He was wrapped up in me coming out, losing a son. I'm not stupid. I knew he realized that was the end of the line for the French family. And he had this way of acknowledging and not fighting who I was, while, at the same time disapproving."

Shaun picked up on one thing in particular. "He does know gay couples can have kids, right?"

Connor looked at him and the way the moonlight fell on his face, and the stubble on his chin, and the quirk of his full lips… God, he looked gorgeous.

"In his world no. But I know that." He had an almost wistful smile. "I'd like kids some day. You?"

Shaun buried a hand in the sand and pulled up a handful, allowing it to escape through his fingers. "One day." He wasn't up to meaningful talks about children, or anything remotely similar at this moment. "You were saying…"

"Oscar, my grandfather, he wants this story stopped. Can't see the value in pulling the story out of the past and making it something it wasn't," he said. The last part was with a gruff accent and Shaun had to assume that was what Oscar French sounded like. Then his voice returned to normal. "He sent me here to shut it down."

Shaun stretched his legs out in front of him, keeping his mouth shut. Part of his work, or research, was to sit and listen, and despite the fuzz in his brain this was good stuff.

"Annalisa, on the other hand, wants to know that Peter and Alfie were happy."

"She does?" Shaun knew he sounded surprised. She'd never got back to him so he assumed she was in the same camp as the rest of the French Foundation. "She supports the book?"

Connor shook his head. "She didn't say she wanted you to write a book, just to see if the man she was married to had been happy."

"So where does this leave us, 'cause you know I'm writing the story."

"I know you are," Connor said. For the first time since they first met he didn't sound pissed and wordy. He seemed resigned. "But how about this? I get you an interview with Annalisa if you let us read the book first."

"First?" Shaun was wary. He'd seen this kind of thing before where there were clauses and legal shit that ended up burying a story. "This is my story as well," he injected so Connor knew what he was playing with.

Connor sighed heavily. "First. Before you find someone to publish it. We need to know you're not the kind of person who sensationalizes; that you'll treat it with respect. Annalisa pointed out that we should work with you, not against you. I'm inclined to agree to see if you're a good man and we can trust you to tell the story accurately."

"So where do we start? I have the first few chapters drafted. Would you...look..." Shaun focused on his words so he could string an entire coherent sentence together. "If you're serious about collaborating, we should have something in writing." Shaun was quite proud of that. He felt abruptly grown up about this situation and it helped that Connor nodded his agreement.

"I'll get something drawn up." Then Connor stood, brushing sand from his pants, small grains flicking at Shaun's face. "Sorry," Connor apologized. He held out a hand to help Shaun up which Shaun took, grateful for any assist to his feet. He rocked up and sideways, Connor steadying him and, for a second, they were right up in each other's space, no more than a breath from each other.

"There's something magical in this place," Shaun whispered. "I don't understand it, but do you feel it? You think Alfie and Peter felt it?" He swayed closer and Connor gripped his upper arms.

Connor chuckled. "I think you're drunk."

The moment passed. Shaun stepped back and steadied himself. "Yep, pretty much."

"I hope you remember this in the morning."

Shaun had lost the filter between brain and mouth. He leaned in. "I remember everything you've ever said," he said. Then he clapped a hand over his mouth. That was way too much information to throw at Connor. "Night," Shaun added. Then he walked away, grabbed his shoes on his way back to the hotel, and fumbled with the keys as he attempted to get into his room. Finally with the door between him and Connor he felt safe.

Safe from what he didn't know but his heart was beating fast like he'd outrun something on the beach. He knew damn well what it was.

Attraction.

Chapter Nine

Connor sat down next to Dylan and opened the folder on the desk, pulling out the items he'd been given that were Peter's. He and Shaun had agreed at a subdued breakfast to meet in Dylan's office later that morning, giving each a chance to organize their thoughts. Connor imagined that Dylan was in the role of mediator.

Actually, today Connor and Shaun planned to collaborate. Shaun emailed over the first two chapters of the story after breakfast, before leaving to have a shower. Connor had to pull his thoughts back to the matter at hand and not focus on Shaun in the shower.

He read the words Shaun had written, which was an awful lot of scene setting concerning Peter and Alfie and the kind of world they were born into. The writing was good, compelling, and Connor was sucked in. Now it was eleven and time to share what he had with Shaun and Dylan, although he wasn't convinced what he had would shed light on anything important.

Shaun came in and took the seat opposite with a

murmured good morning, and two days of stubble now. He didn't look worse the wear for last night's cocktails, but he wouldn't look Connor in the eyes. Exactly the same as at breakfast.

"I read the chapters," Connor said. What he thought of them may well be enough to break the ice. Shaun did meet his eyes then, but he looked wary. "I really liked them."

"Thank you," Shaun said.

Then there was silence. Connor looked at Dylan and Dylan shrugged. "Coffee," Dylan announced. "Back in five."

"What's wrong?" Connor asked as soon as he left.

"Just embarrassed. Don't know half of what I was saying last night. Should I apologize?"

"You already did that once." Connor offered a smile which Shaun returned. "Anyway, look at this, your chapter two said no one would know on the island but…" Connor thumbed through the beaten-up notebook of Peter's, found the place and turned it to face Shaun.

Shaun traced the words with a finger hovering just above the paper, then sat back in the chair. "The staff knew."

"Seems to me everyone knew. Like Sapphire Cay was some kind of safe place for those that could afford it. And we know Peter had money."

"That throws a whole new light on things." Shaun pointed at the bottom corner of the entry. "The same tiny shell picture." The shell or variations of it, had appeared on letters, ones from both Alfie and Peter, their journals, and sketches from the three sources. Some of the drawings were more like idle doodles in scraps of space. Half looked professionally drawn, the others a little less perfect. Shaun liked to believe the men both drew them; one an artist, the other copying the style, and that between them they had a code of sorts.

Dylan returned with coffee and placed it and a plate of cookies on the table. "Okay?" he asked.

"We need a timeline," Shaun said with a decisive nod. He pulled clean lined paper toward him and scribbled dates down the left-hand side from the thirties to the sixties. Then he added two headings, one for Alfie, one for Peter.

Together the three men looked at letters and by the time Scott passed in a huge plate of bread, meats, and cheeses, they had a cohesive timeline.

"So we know Alfie was called up."

Dylan followed. "He served in the Pacific."

"And he survived the war, staying in the UK and marrying an English girl who died in childbirth. A few years later he returned to the States with his son." Connor paused. This was Shaun's great-great-grandmother they were discussing, but he couldn't think of a more tactful way to summarize.

Dylan pointed at the list of dates. "And he died in the fall of 1966, aged forty-nine, from cancer."

"And we know Peter didn't fight but worked with the French Foundation in the POW camps in the US. Also before that in 1942 he and Annalisa divorced."

Shaun sighed. "There were no letters after Alfie went to war. We know he got married; I assume he decided to make a life that was easier? No one in the family knows much about him." He pulled out a sheet of paper. "My grandfather James was born in 1946, and all he used to say was that his dad was a war hero and that he died when James himself was in the army. For all intents and purposes Alfie seemed like a bit of an absent father. My dad often talks about how granddad wanted to be different."

"So it's almost a blank in the intervening years, all apart from this letter sent December 1965." Connor centered the letter in the middle of the table. "Dearest P, I had some dreadful news, and all I could think was that I needed you. How silly is that after all this time. I will be at the waterfall, around the end of May, early June. Yours. Then there is no signatory, just the small shell."

He studied the shell. It's design was simpler than most of the others, the style and impressions of the pencil different somehow. If Alfie was the artist, then Connor guessed illness might have hindered his creativity and skill. But in his heart he believed the sketches he had were drawn by Peter. He couldn't explain what it was that had him so sure. He just was.

"And Peter kept this letter," Shaun said.

Connor nodded. Then he placed a hand on the journal. "So all we have now are the words about the meet in 1966. When Peter was here with Alfie again."

Shaun pushed up and away from the table. "I don't want to hear them now," he announced. "I think I'm going to get some air."

"It's raining," Dylan nodded at the window where rain tracked down the glass.

Shaun shrugged, "I can handle rain."

Connor didn't want to let Shaun leave like this.

Something in what they were doing here was resonating with Shaun and he was visibly drained. Not surprising really, Shaun was the one creating a whole novel out of this.

"Can you handle company?" Connor asked.

Shaun smiled and nodded. The two men left the hotel, the rain soft on their skin, and they followed a natural path away from the central area and between trees. The Cay wasn't very big and Dylan had indicated the general direction of the waterfall; the one mentioned so many times in the letters, and featured in a couple of the photos.

"Did Dylan tell you he and his partner found the box under the shack by the waterfall after the island caught the edge of a big storm last year?"

"Yeah. What were the chances that would happen?" They came to a fork in the path and Shaun stopped, tilting his head like he was getting his bearings. Connor stopped next to him.

"Which way do you think?" Connor asked.

"I say right."

"You have a better handle on the geography of this island than I do."

"Yeah," Shaun said, then grinned. "Let's go this way; has to be down here somewhere."

They walked companionably for about five minutes. The trees thinned before the turn opened to a full crescent bay and right at its apex a stunning rock formation with water pouring into it from a natural spring.

Connor strode straight over, kicking off his shoes and pushing off his pants and tee, climbing the short tumble of rocks to slip into the water in just his jersey boxers. The rain was still falling, great huge drops that sent little spirals of water up as they connected with the pool at the foot of the short waterfall. He slipped beneath the water and allowed the coldness of it to wash over his head. For a while, he held his breath then pushed off the sandy bottom and broke through the surface to the warm and close outside. He thought Shaun might have joined him, but the man stood a little distance away with his hands pushed into his jeans.

"Come in, it's gorgeous."

Shaun moved a little closer, but he didn't look convinced. "It's cold isn't it?"

Connor rubbed at the goosebumps on his arms then ducked under again. When he surfaced, he knew he had the widest grin. "No. Come on."

Shaun was now right up close. The only thing between him and the water was the retaining walls of stones and the earth pressed up against them. "I can't swim," he said.

"Really?" Connor couldn't believe anyone in this day and age couldn't swim.

"I mean, I can swim," Shaun amended, "but I don't because I am scared and I panic."

"You can come in here. It's maybe four feet," Connor stood up to prove it. "And I can see the bottom, it's so clear."

Shaun climbed the wall and sat on the side with his bare feet dangling in the cold water. "This is as far as I go."

Connor swam over to him, trying to tread water, but this water really was not deep enough so he kind of stood-crouched and the water was over his shoulders. Lazily he balanced there and tilted his head to the rain.

"You think they were happy?" Shaun asked.

Connor looked back at Shaun, at the large patches of wet where the rain hit his tee. He looked pensive and stunning at the same time. "They were in love. The times they stole, they were happy, I think." He dipped his chin under the water. "Have you ever been in love?" Connor asked. He'd already admitted he had never been in love, but part of him wanted to know if Shaun had. Just so he could judge how much of an aberration he *actually* was.

"Once." Shaun smiled fondly. "His name was Ian and we were sixteen. We outed each other by accident after a sports lesson." The smile fell. "Anyway. This is the waterfall then."

"When you see the photographs, it's obviously the place." He swam a little closer and gripped the rocks that Shaun sat on before standing up. The move had him right between Shaun's spread legs although no part of either man was touching. If Shaun was startled he didn't show it, he just looked at Connor with a steady gaze.

Unbidden Connor moved his hand so it rested on Shaun's knee. "You think this place has magic?"

Shaun smiled at him. There was no verbal answer. The smile was enough. Connor moved a little closer, the rain falling on them, heavier now.

"Shaun. Do you feel this?" Connor had never said words like this before, never asked such a question, but the attraction between them… He couldn't have misread that? Could he?

Shaun reached out and curled Connor's hair behind his ear. "The magic," he whispered.

Connor was hard at that simple touch, an electrical impulse that seemed to short-circuit his brain until there was only emotion left. "Can I kiss you?"

They were centimeters apart, Connor blocked by stone to get any traction, and Shaun leaned forward to close the distance. The first kiss was soft and searching, close-mouthed they pressed lips together with a quiet peace that was the most passionate touch Connor had ever felt. He moaned low in his throat and Shaun seemed just as affected. He curled his hands around Shaun's head, used the pressure there to angle the kiss, then the touch deepened. For the longest time, they kissed at the pool. Until the rain became so heavy that it made breathing through the kiss awkward. They separated and with unspoken agreement Shaun moved to pick up Connor's soaked clothes while Connor climbed out of the pool. They ran to the trees, and Shaun didn't complain when Connor took his hand.

They walked back to the hotel talking softly about Alfie and Peter. Then took shelter inside the back steps watching lightning split the vast sky.

Chapter Ten

THERE SHE IS.

Lucas looked fondly across the horizon as he neared Sapphire Cay.

Home.

He didn't think he had ever been away from the island and Dylan at the same time for this long before. Since he moved out here to be with Dylan, he couldn't remember a time they had been apart and him feeling it. Though the reason for having to leave him behind had been an important one, he would be glad to set his feet on the sands of home and have his husband wrap his arms around him. Though he wished Dylan could have made the trip with him, he appreciated life at the Cay didn't just stop because his sister had given birth, even if the birth was early.

Tasha had just passed thirty-five weeks. Lucas had scared himself with plenty of articles on the internet about the difficulties a premature birth could bring with it for the baby; for the baby's breathing, feeding, staying warm. It didn't matter how many times Liam had assured him on the phone. Or the fact Dylan had repeated Liam's words over and over. Mother and baby were fine, both were healthy, and Francesca was the most perfect little girl in the whole world. Lucas couldn't help but worry. He wasn't going to stop worrying until he had seen his sister and new baby niece with his own eyes.

From the moment he set eyes on baby Francesca, he was in love. She was adorable, from her tiny fingers and toes to her squashed but cute button nose. From the heart-melting way her mouth curled into what looked like a smile as she slept, to the way her right ear stuck out from her head that little bit more than the left. To him, to her parents and grandmother, she was perfect.

Having gotten the first flight he could, Lucas had stayed with his sister for eleven days. Long enough to see Tasha and the baby back home and settled. Francesca was beautiful, strong and loud. Just like her mother.

Breathing in the cool air, Lucas tapped his hand to the pocket of his board shorts, content when he felt his cell phone. He had messaged Dylan with a picture, but he couldn't wait to share the others he had taken. He must have gotten broody for roughly ten minutes. Then there had been crying and pooping. He was content and proud to simply have his new title as Uncle Lucas.

With a smile on his face, he glanced up at the white clouds overhead, squinting at the white light despite his sunglasses. It was June, the summer season out there in the Bahamas, and with summer came muggy heat, rain and storms. Just the other night, when he had been on the phone to Dylan, he had heard the rumble of thunder down the line. It had been strangely comforting, knowing things were exactly how they should be, home on the island.

Lucas focused on Sapphire Cay.

Not long now.

He eyed the beach and pier. He knew exactly who was waiting for him on the wooden dock. There was something instantly recognizable about his husband and the way he was standing with his arms folded across his broad chest, the slight bend of his knee as he rested his weight on his other leg.

Easing off the lever, Lucas reduced his speed and steered Liberty Two toward the pier.

Scott was right in his email. We need a better name.

In his time out on the Cay, he had learned enough about boats to be safe. If anything unthinkable happened, he could get him and Dylan, or any of their staff and guests over to Marsh Harbor if he needed to. He wasn't what he would call a natural when it came to being at the helm of a boat. He was constantly going over the instructions Dylan had given him in his head, calmly going through each step in the process from starting the engine through to docking at his destination. When Dylan had asked him to bring the new boat to Sapphire Cay, Lucas had been a little surprised. As it seemed the original Liberty had a few *issues*, it was probably the better option. Dylan had insisted Lucas didn't have to bring back the boat if he didn't feel okay about it. He said he and Scott would figure something out. Lucas had been left with a picture of Lady Liberty cutting out in the middle of nowhere, Dylan and Scott drifting away.

Lucas went through the guide in his head, ticking off

the stages as he closed in on the dock. Up until that point, he had been pretty confident he could get Liberty Two from A to B. But now he found himself with an audience.

Scott was standing where the pier met the sand, talking to a man who wasn't Adam. The way the man held himself was familiar to Lucas, all business and formal. He'd looked like that once, before Dylan and Sapphire Cay had worked its magic. He figured from the air of authority that man was Connor French.

No pressure.

He cut the engine, letting Liberty Two carry herself forward under her own momentum. When he was close enough, he threw the line to Dylan.

Dylan was wearing a broad smile as he stepped forward. "Any problems?" Dylan asked, bending down to tie up the boat.

"No, none." Lucas grabbed his pack and threw it out onto the pier. He held out his hand and Dylan helped him step up and out. It took a moment for Lucas to get used to being back on stable ground. "She ran fine. Sounded great. I have all the parts you ordered." He didn't give Dylan a chance to ask anything else. He cupped Dylan's face and pulled him into a firm kiss. Lucas sighed as he breathed in the scent he had missed for the last eleven days. The scent that was wholly Dylan, mixed with the ocean, the trace of mechanical grease from having worked on Lady Liberty, and the fresh fruity smell of his shampoo.

"I missed you, too." Dylan hugged Lucas tightly. "How is everyone?"

"They're okay, actually they're great. You should have seen them. A proper little family."

Dylan loosened his hold. He had a look in his eyes, some misplaced sympathy. "They're still your family too."

Lucas pressed his palm to Dylan's cheek. He glanced past him at Scott, then to where Mutt was running circles in the sand. "Of course they are. But I have plenty of family right here." There would always be that bond with Tasha, and just like these last eleven days, he would always be there for her if she needed him. But she was a mother now and moving on to the next chapter in her life. For Lucas, his future lay with Dylan and this island, their marriage, and their business.

Quirking an eyebrow, Lucas watched Mutt bound over to a man sitting in the shade of the line of trees. He watched for a moment as who he guessed was Shaun Jamieson stroked Mutt, then tossed a stick several feet away from him for Mutt to collect.

"Mutt made a new friend," Dylan stated, picking up Lucas's bag.

"So I see." Lucas was hit with a pang of jealousy, though only briefly. "Have our guests behaved themselves?"

Dylan had mostly skirted around the fact he had gone ahead, despite Lucas's warnings, and agreed to host parties representing both families invested in the Peter/Alfie relationship.

"They're getting along?" Lucas raised his voice a little as he asked the question.

"Yeah. Look." Dylan indicated behind him.

Connor was still standing with Scott, deep in conversation over something Lucas couldn't hear from this distance, and Shaun was wearing a smitten face as he petted Mutt behind the ears.

Sure they're getting along. If getting along means keeping them apart.

He dipped his head and looked over the top of his shades. The look he shot Dylan did the trick, and Dylan dropped his shoulders as he made a confession.

"Fine. Maybe it doesn't look like it. Okay, sure they didn't get off on the right foot to begin with. But I swear they've been talking and have been nothing but civil to one another these last couple of days."

Lucas screwed up his mouth as he looked between the two men. He liked to know where everybody stood. "Do you know what they've decided about Peter and Alfie's story?" Though he hoped the romance between the two men wouldn't be hidden away back inside the old biscuit tin, he did understand how people, family, might want to see it forgotten about. It wasn't his or Dylan's place to get involved, not really, and the last thing he wanted was them and Sapphire Cay being dragged into some legal battle.

Dylan glanced over his shoulder and gave a little shrug. "Well, from what I gather, Shaun can write his book, but whether it's published, that will be down to Connor and his family. See if they approve, I guess."

"That's got to be good, right? There's a chance their story will make it off the island." He squeezed Dylan's wrist as he was filled with optimism and a sense of pride in having had a hand in the love story being unearthed quite literally.

"Yeah. Yeah, it is." Dylan smiled a bright smile and Lucas was glad to be home.

Blinking, Lucas freed himself from the spell Dylan had seemingly put him under, drawing his gaze from Dylan's gorgeous mouth. "Okay. Well, I should probably go introduce myself." He stepped away from Dylan.

"Lucas," Dylan called after him.

Lucas turned around. "Yeah—" He closed his eyes as Dylan pressed his mouth to his in a firm kiss.

"Missed ya," Dylan said cheerfully, then trotted off ahead.

Snorting a laugh, Lucas followed after him.

It's good to be home.

———

"THE WIND'S PICKING UP OUT THERE," DYLAN SAID, dropping down on the couch beside Lucas.

"Uh-huh," Lucas said. He was leaning over the coffee table, reading through some handwritten notes Dylan recognized as being some of those Shaun had brought with him.

"I've made a start on locking this place down, but with Scott working on Lady Liberty, I could do with a hand."

Lucas didn't answer. Instead, he shuffled pages around.

"He wants to be out of here in a few days now he has that placement and a contract all drawn up."

Scott had stayed between Sapphire Cay and Miami last year as there had been work lined up for him. But this year, he was determined to head back out to the botanical gardens in Singapore and take Adam with him.

Dylan sighed and picked at a loose thread on the arm of the couch. "The news reports say there're some pretty severe storms heading our way. There's the patio to remove, structures to double-check, a few hatches left to batten down." He smirked, but was left disappointed when Lucas paid him no attention. "I thought I might give Shaun a hammer and have him lend a hand."

Lucas gave a slow nod. "Okay."

"Or we could dress Connor up like a unicorn and have him do a dance to appease the storm gods."

Lifting his head, Lucas glanced at Dylan. He pursed his lips and shot him a despairing look. "I was listening, you know?"

"Of course you were." Dylan sat back and folded his arms across his chest.

Lucas snorted a laugh. "Are you sulking?"

"No." Dylan couldn't help but smile. "I'm not sulking. I'm just..." He shrugged.

"Aww, are you feeling lonely and ignored?" Lucas said in a teasing voice.

"Pfft. No."

Once Lucas had unpacked, he had immersed himself in the history of the love affair and the copies of the letters Shaun had brought with him. Though Dylan admitted it was all kind of cool making these connections with dates and both sets of notes, he had hoped for a bit of together time.

Leaning back his head, Dylan ran his tongue over his teeth and sighed. "Okay, maybe a little." He eyed the fanned-out pages of notes. "I feel like I've lost you to paper."

Lucas placed the pages on the table. He wore an *as-if* expression when he looked at Dylan. "This?" He held up a sheet then tossed it away. The paper spun upward, flipping over itself as it changed direction and hit Lucas in the chest.

Laughter erupted from Dylan and he wrapped his hand around the back of Lucas's neck, pulling him into a kiss. "That didn't go to plan, did it?"

Lucas shuffled closer. "The gesture was there." He cupped Dylan's face, leaning into him and edging him backward against the cushion of the couch. He gave a soft sigh as he kissed Dylan and curled his fingers down through Dylan's hair. "I missed you."

Dylan sank lower on the cushion, and Lucas rested against his chest. He closed his eyes and lost himself in the warmth of his husband pressing against him. Running his hand down Lucas's spine, Dylan groaned with desire. *God, how I had missed this, the touching, the kissing.* Eleven days had never felt so long. He wished he had the words to tell Lucas how much he meant to him. A simple 'I love you' seemed too little. With one hand, he held Lucas's face, pulled him close. With the other, Dylan cupped his ass and squeezed.

With a laugh, Lucas lifted his head and looked down at Dylan.

Their eyes met and Dylan was struck by the most intense feeling of joy. "I do love you. You know that right?"

Lucas held Dylan by the chin and grinned. "Of course I know." He guided Dylan forward and kissed him soundly on the mouth. There was a flare of mischief in Lucas's eyes and Dylan groaned when Lucas found his way inside the front of his cut-offs with stealthy ease.

"Lu—" Dylan grunted as Lucas closed his hand around his cock. "Fuck." He closed his eyes as Lucas kissed him again. Apart from Connor and Shaun, the Cay was closed for the season to vacationers and wedding parties, and it was moments like this he was looking forward to. Just him and Lucas. Nobody to run around after or to steal away their time. Just the two of them.

He took deep, steady breaths and leaned his head back. Lucas pressed kisses across his collarbone, a kiss for each stroke of his fist over Dylan's dick. He trailed his kisses higher until their mouths met in an open-mouthed kiss. Dylan breathed soft sounds on Lucas's lips and wrapped his hand around the back of Lucas's neck.

So close.

Thoughts of Lucas naked, straddling him, riding him, played out in Dylan's head. Fuck, he wanted more. He lifted his hips, jabbing upward into every downward stroke Lucas made. He spread his legs, his body tensing. Tightening his hold on Lucas, he opened his mouth, awkwardly kissing between grunted breaths as he reached his climax.

Oh fuck. He jerked roughly upward as he came. The noise of his orgasm was muted by Lucas's mouth on his.

Lucas gently brought the moment to an end with a few short tugs of Dylan's dick. After a firm kiss, he leaned back and withdrew his hand. With a sigh, he settled against the cushions of the couch and stared up at the ceiling. He smiled and rolled his head to look at Dylan. Lucas didn't say anything for a moment, merely stared at Dylan with love in his eyes.

"Better?" Lucas said.

Dylan gave a breathy laugh and glanced down at the bulge in the front of his open shorts. "Better," he said.

Lucas's smile brightened.

"God, I missed you." Dylan sat forward and planted a kiss on Lucas's mouth. "Don't ever go away for that long again."

Reaching up, Lucas gently smoothed his hand over Dylan's face and kissed him. "Not planning on it. Now go clean up. We still have guests."

Dylan nodded.

Only a couple more days and they would have the island to themselves again.

He couldn't wait.

Chapter Eleven

"Fuck." Connor flinched as a stray branch blew across the patio and hit the half-shuttered window. It was just a storm. Only wind and rain, albeit dramatic wind and rain. He narrowed his eyes, ducking his head to get a better view of the darkening sky.

"Hey," a gruff voice came from behind him.

Connor turned and quirked an eyebrow at the sight of Scott. The man was a vision of windswept dark hair and clinging wet material. His mind went places it shouldn't. "Um, yeah?"

"Your friend? You know where he's at?" Scott was straight to the point. He sniffed and shook his head, water running down his cheek from his hair.

"Shaun?" Connor's eyes drifted lower to Scott's equally wet and equally clinging board shorts.

Scott turned his body slightly, as if aware of exactly what had Connor's interest. "Yeah, Shaun. Skinny guy. Dark hair. Good with animals." There was a palpable tension in Scott's voice.

"I don't know. Is everything okay?" he added quickly. Connor couldn't figure out if it was him Scott had a problem with, or if it could be something else.

It was like a switch was flipped and the look on Scott's face softened. "Sorry, sorry." He took a deep breath and seemed to find a slice of calm when he spoke to Connor. "It's the weather. Makes me a little crazy sometimes." He glanced at the window.

"This is normal, right? We're safe here, aren't we?" When his grandfather had insisted he fly out to Sapphire Cay after Shaun had come to the office, Connor had done a little digging where the weather was concerned out in the Bahamas and at Sapphire Cay. He was well aware they were in the wet season and with it came storms and hurricanes.

"What? Yeah, yeah. We're all set... Mostly." Scott ran a hand back through his hair. "Look. Everything's fine. This place has been standing more years than you've had cocktail parties." There was a twinkle in Scott's eyes and Connor got the distinct impression the cocktail party reference was a dig at the fact he came from money.

You work for a guy who owns a freaking island.

"How bad can it get? There's a scale or something, right?"

Scott rested his hands on his hips and shrugged. "For hurricanes, yeah. But the season varies year to year. Most of the time it's just muggy heat and lots of rain, some thunder, and lightning. High winds, you know, the tail end of the hurricane type stuff. Don't get me wrong, hurricanes can affect us. But it's not all bad, I mean you might not be here if it wasn't for last year."

Connor narrowed his eyes.

"Dislodging the ground by the shack. It meant Dylan and Lucas found that old tin of your great, great...great?" Scott pursed his lips and looked at the puddle of water that had formed around his sneakers. "It meant they found Peter's letters," he settled with.

"Right." Connor glanced at the gap in the shutters. He tilted his head as the sway of the trees outside caught his eye. "Crap."

"What?"

"I just remembered where Shaun is. He took Mutt out." The weather had been fine up until an hour ago. Over the first sixty minutes, the wind had strengthened and light rain showers had turned into thick sheets. Christ, had Shaun really been gone all that time?

Panic gripped Connor's chest. What if something had happened? He watched the trees bowing in the wind, and terrifying thoughts came into his head. The wind could have brought down a tree. Shaun could be lying there trapped, or worse.

"I need to find him." Connor didn't give Scott a chance to argue against his decision, but he heard the muttered curse as Scott fell in behind him.

"MUTT?" SHAUN RAISED HIS HAND TO PROTECT HIS FACE. The wind whipped up sand and spray off the beach.

Damn it.

Shaun held his wet bangs back from his face and looked at the ocean. He steadied himself against the strength of the wind and watched the waves rise angrily into the air before breaking on the shore.

He looked to the horizon at the sound of thunder. He tilted his head, listening as the sound made way for something familiar and relief flooded through him. Turning around, he crouched down and welcomed Mutt in a hug.

"Where have you been?" He stroked Mutt's slick coat.

Shaun had been about to give up, having assumed Mutt probably knew his way around this island better than him and would have headed for safety and home by now. He stroked Mutt's head. "Or did you come back for me?" He held onto Mutt's collar as he stood and checked the tree line. They needed to get back to the hotel.

Mutt lurched forward as white lit the sky in a jagged streak.

"It's okay." Shaun held onto the dog. "Let's get out of here, yeah?" He kept a tight hold on Mutt's collar, just in case, but it seemed Mutt was keen to head home and jerked them both forward to the trees.

Shaun allowed Mutt to guide him through the faux night caused by ominous dark clouds, eventually coming across a path and marker that pointed them back toward the hotel. Shaun took advantage of the most sheltered area to push his hair back from his face and wipe the rain from his cheeks. It was like the weather had come out of nowhere. One minute it was all sunshine and playing with Mutt on the beach, the next it was high winds and intermittent downpours. The first rumble of thunder had spooked Mutt, sending the dog running at full speed across the sand. Shaun hadn't been able to keep up.

Taking a right, they headed up the path and Shaun was relieved to find himself at the gazebo. He stopped at the wooden structure and turned around to view the ocean. The white foam crashing on the beach was amazing. He had never seen anything quite like it. He always thought the people on television chasing twisters and storms were crazy, but to stand here and be completely surrounded by it, it was all kinds of intense and utterly mesmerizing.

And fucking scary.

"Shaun."

The call of his name was muffled by the sound of the wind in his ears and rain on his head, but he was sure he hadn't imagined it. "Come on." He encouraged Mutt up the path to the back of the hotel and welcomed the open space of the patio area. On the far side of the pool, the hatch of the cocktail hut banged in time to the gusts of wind. He was relieved when he caught sight of Connor and Scott.

Scott was saving a white plastic sun lounger, which had been blown onto its side. He struggled with the piece of furniture, managing to maneuver it through the open sliding door leading to the reception area.

"You okay?" Connor shouted. He couldn't have been outside long, his hair, though ruffled by the wind, was dry, and his T-shirt was merely speckled with the rain. "I was worried."

"We took the scenic route." Shaun released Mutt's collar when the dog struggled to free itself from his hold. He watched Mutt run around the pool and inside, nearly tripping Scott as he bounded through the open door. Shaun looked behind him. The tall trees seemed to be part of some hypnotic dance, bowing down to the wind's force.

A strange sound echoed around him that made Shaun stop and look back at the ocean. The sound was unearthly, like nothing he had heard before, and it seemed to come from every direction. Wind blasted against him, strong enough to have him stepping back and needing to brace himself from its force. He heard Connor shouting. It took a moment for him to figure out exactly what the noise had been, but by then it was too late. One of the trees gave out under the strain and came crashing down. Greenery and branches were on top of him, scratching his face as he stumbled backward. He lost his footing and fell sideways. There was an almighty smack as he fell back and suddenly he was swamped by something cold and wet.

No, no, no.

Pool water filled his ears and mouth. Everything was muffled and he grabbed for something, anything as he kicked his legs. He didn't know which way was up and which was down.

Fuck. Fuck. Where's the side? Where's the surface?

He couldn't think straight. His clothes clung to him, dragged him down like heavy weights. The splatters of green and brown of debris from the fallen tree mixed with bubbles as he thrashed in the water. He was fucked. Something tight gripped his shoulder; a burst of pain as he was dragged sideways. Gasping, he broke the surface. He slapped the water with his hands as he tried to keep his head out of the water.

"Straighten your legs." Connor was in the pool beside him, holding Shaun's face and brushing back his hair.

"Hey." He gripped Shaun's head and forced him to focus on him. "Straighten your legs," he said firmly.

Shaun kept his eyes on Connor and nodded, blowing the water from his mouth as he briefly dipped back under up to his nose. He extended his legs, the toe of his shoe scuffing something solid ever so briefly.

"The bottom is there, okay?" Connor was treading water beside him. "That's as deep as it gets." He blew away the water that had collected on his upper lip. "You calm?"

I'm calm. I trust you.

Shaun nodded again as he tried to catch his breath and paddle to keep himself afloat at the same time. He was cold, but he was okay. He wasn't lost at sea with sharks circling him. He hadn't ventured out onto a frozen lake and fallen through the ice, his only escape freezing over. He wasn't that four-year-old boy who capsized his inflatable fish-shaped boat on a family day at the beach and nearly drowned. He was okay. He wasn't alone. He was a grown fucking man.

"Take my hand." Connor reached out to Shaun, and Shaun quickly took his hand. He gulped in a deep breath as he sank beneath the surface, but Connor was holding him tightly, pulling on his arm and raising him up.

Connor stayed facing Shaun, swimming backward until Shaun let out a small but joyous cry.

"I can touch the bottom."

Connor didn't let go of his hand, despite them both being able to stand, the water level coming up to just above their stomachs. Hand in hand they made their way to the edge, where Scott was standing to help pull them up out of the water.

"You okay?" Scott asked. He looked worriedly between Shaun and Connor.

Wiping at his face, Shaun managed a nod. He winced as his fingers traced slight, raised lines where the trees branched must have sliced his face. "I'm all right."

Shook up like hell. But fine.

"Let's get you inside and cleaned up." Connor was still holding Shaun's hand.

Shaun let Connor guide him to the door. Stepping into the reception area, Shaun couldn't stop himself from shivering. Maybe he was cold, or maybe it was the shock, but it was like he had no control over his body.

Wearing a comforting smile, Connor stood in front of him. He finally released Shaun's hand to instead caress Shaun's shoulders. "That was a bit dramatic." He looked at Shaun's face, seeming to wince on Shaun's behalf as he checked the scratches. "Maybe you could put it in a book."

Shaun drew his eyebrows together and stared at Connor. Connor curled down his mouth and looked awkward. There was a beat, then Shaun laughed. "If it's okay with you, I'd prefer if we kept it just between us." He sat down on the sun lounger he had seen Scott wrestling with before and glanced over his shoulder when the room darkened a little.

"Okay. We're as secure as we're going to get right now," said Scott, ducking to get under the shutter he had half-rolled down. "It's getting crazy out there." He pushed down firmly on the screen until it met the ground then closed the patio door.

There was a strange howling sound, accompanied by the pitter-patter of rain against the shutter.

"Is this a hurricane?" Shaun hugged himself. He was soaked through.

Scott shrugged. "Maybe. Worst storm I've seen out here."

"Global warming," Adam said and turned on a light. "That's what everyone blames, right?" Adam stopped and looked at Shaun. "Are you okay? You look terrible."

Shaun opened his mouth but didn't say anything at first.

"Nice one," Scott grumbled.

Adam let out an *oomph* as he was hit in the face with Scott's wet T-shirt. "Asshole."

Shaun glanced at the very broad- and very bare-chested Scott. The man had an amazing tan. *I wonder if he has white bits.* Then he looked back at Connor and realized he didn't actually care when Connor stood there looking all battered and heroic.

Clearing his throat, Shaun insisted, "I'm okay. Nothing a warm shower won't fix."

"Do you have any antiseptic or wipes for Shaun's face? Just to get him cleaned up," Connor asked.

"Sure," Scott said. "Just give me a second." He grabbed Adam by the arm and dragged him toward the office and private living space Lucas and Dylan had attached to the hotel. Scott was whispering, loud and urgent, and Adam looked taken aback as Scott was apparently filling him in on the events of only a moment ago.

"I need to take that shower." Shaun stood up, surprised

when Connor was at his side. "I'm okay," he assured him. "Honestly."

"I know." Connor soothed his hand over Shaun's forearm. "But I'm going to come with you. And you can protest all you like, but it's going to happen. Let me look after you."

They stood together, looking into each other's eyes until a small cough broke the spell between them.

"Antiseptic liquid. Q-tips." Adam handed them over to Connor. "Oh and a pack of Reese's Peanut Butter Cups." He pulled the candy from his shirt pocket. When neither man took candy, he apologized. "Sorry. Are you allergic? Peanuts. Some people are, aren't they? I didn't think."

"No. Well, I'm not." Shaun looked at Connor. "You?"

Connor shook his head.

Shaun smiled and held out his hand. A sugar fix might help his nerves, assuming he could shake the feeling of nausea that had settled in his stomach. "Thanks."

Flashing a smile, Adam gave Shaun the candy then excused himself.

Scott closed the last of the blinds in the hallway. "Keep your shutters closed, and listen for an alarm, if the storm becomes worse we'll need to move into the shelter and I'll sound the alarm."

"You have a shelter?" *And an alarm?*

"Just be aware, if the storm increases…" Scott didn't have to say anything else.

Shaun wasn't feeling the love for a hurricane shelter. Thankfully, Connor interrupted his spiraling thoughts after the pool incident.

"Come on, let's get you cleaned up," Connor prompted.

With a sigh, Shaun did as he was told. He was exhausted.

The next few minutes Shaun walked through in some kind of daze. They stopped off at Connor's room so he could grab a towel and change of clothes. Before he knew it, he was in his room, Connor urging him into the en-suite and pushing a towel against his chest. He tried protesting, but Connor insisted he would be there when Shaun was done. Too tired to argue, Shaun pushed the door to the bathroom closed, then stripped. He threw his wet clothes in the sink and checked his face in the mirror as best he could in the dim light. The left side of his face was littered with scratches. None looked particularly deep, but the sharp branches had drawn blood. The longest of the marks ran from below his ear to just short of his mouth. The wound looked raised and raw. He opened his mouth, mimicked chewing. To his relief, it didn't hurt.

Breathing in deeply, he turned away from the mirror. He was fine and there was no serious damage except to his shredded nerves. A shower, a drink, and a nap were what he needed. Stepping into the bath, he pulled the shower curtain and turned on the water.

Step one. Shower.

GOD, IT FEELS GOOD TO BE DRY.

Connor sat at the end of the bed in his towel and listened to the sound of the shower. It was so nice to be out of his wet clothes and he felt halfway to human again. Outside the wind was howling as it blew through gaps in the shutters. All he could think about was Shaun and thank God he was okay. The moment had been like something out of some disaster movie. When Shaun had fallen into the water, Connor's mind had gone straight to the other night; recalling the fact that Shaun was afraid of the water and could barely swim. His mind had clicked into some action mode and he had been wading in to help.

Closing his eyes, he blew out a breath. He tried to think about something else, about Shaun and the magic of the waterfall. But the beautiful memory was tarnished with thoughts of *what-if*. Connor opened his eyes and got to his feet. Making sure his towel was wrapped tight and secure, he walked over to the dresser where Shaun's journal, crammed with notes about Peter and Alfie, was resting. Hesitantly, he picked up the bound pages, and carefully thumbed through, randomly opening the page. He cocked his head as he scrolled through the almost illegible script.

He turned over some more pages until he came to the last entry that had been made as part of the timeline. Shaun had been compiling when Peter and Alfie had spent time together or exchanged letters. What notes Connor could make out, were commentary about the end of Peter and Alfie's story when Alfie had died.

They had spent so many years apart, only to meet up again in 1966 for one last summer, detailed in a letter that was in Shaun's bundle from his great-grandfather. The summer before Alfie had died. There had been a storm then as well, one that ripped trees and caused a lot of damage. Were Peter and Alfie as nervous about the destructive forces as Shaun was? *Was that last summer a goodbye?*

Unsettled, Connor glanced at the closed door. He wondered if Peter had regretted anything in the end. Did he regret not going to Alfie sooner? Did he wish they'd had longer? Did he treasure the time they had had? Or maybe he had hoped they'd never met at all? Never started something that could only have brought with it heartache and pain? Were the final few moments they managed to share some cruel torment? Or, did they give them their happy ending?

The sound of Shaun opening the bathroom door startled Connor from his thoughts. He closed the journal and put it back on the dresser. Turning around, he leaned back and waited.

Shaun stepped out, a towel fastened around his waist, his dark hair wet and pushed back from his face and his cheeks and chest red from the heat of the water and steam.

"Feeling better?" Connor said.

"Yes. Thank you." Shaun blew a breath and sat down on the bed. "I could really do with a drink." He held his hands out in front of him, scrutinizing them.

Connor brought the antiseptic and Q-tips with him and sat down beside Shaun. He eyed Shaun's hands. They were trembling. "How about I check over those cuts, then I'll see what I can do?" He could get Shaun beer, maybe himself one too.

"Okay." Shaun sat up straight and slightly tilted his head. "They didn't look that bad in the mirror."

The shutters rattled outside the window, together with the sound of rain being blown against the side of the hotel.

Connor paused briefly, expecting to hear the alarm, but didn't hear anything.

He shuffled closer and gently touched Shaun's face, holding his chin as he angled his face from side to side. The branches had drawn blood in some places. Carefully, he poured some of the liquid into the cap and handed it to Shaun to hold. He took a Q-tip and dipped it in the liquid.

"Hold still. This might sting." Narrowing his eyes, he gently drew the cotton swab along the length of one of the deeper cuts.

Shaun's cheek twitched and Connor apologized. He met Shaun's eyes and swallowed hard. Did Shaun feel it too? The intense desire to touch, to hold, to kiss?

"It's fine. Just carry on." Shaun closed his eyes and relaxed his face. If he had felt anything, he seemed able to dismiss those feelings.

Disappointment pricked at Connor's heart.

What did you expect to happen? Shaun falling into your arms just because you played hero?

Connor tended to Shaun's injuries, coating a handful of cuts in the liquid until he was satisfied. Taking the lid and the used cotton swabs, he cleared up, then returned to sit next to Shaun.

"I dare any of those cuts to even think about getting infected." He made the joke, then fell into an awkward silence. He looked at the floor, surprised when Shaun rested his hand on his knee. He turned his head and met Shaun's gorgeous light blue eyes. In them, he saw gratitude.

"Thank you," Shaun said. He didn't move his hand as he locked his gaze with Connor's. Beneath the gratitude was something more, a hunger, like Connor felt for Shaun. Shaun made a rushed move. He cupped Connor's face and dragged him into a firm kiss.

Heat spread through Connor as he reached up and held Shaun steady. The kiss was rough but full of lustful want. Shaun slipped his tongue into Connor's mouth and Connor groaned around the muscle, pushing back with his own tongue as he threaded his fingers through Connor's hair. He smiled into the kiss as Shaun lowered his hands, pressing them to his chest, running them up and over his shoulders.

Shaun caught Connor's lower lip between his teeth, sucking hard before releasing it. He leaned back and locked eyes with Connor for a moment, though Connor didn't know what Shaun was hoping to see.

"I must be mad," Shaun declared. He didn't give Connor the chance to reply, and there he was in Connor's space, encouraging him to lie back on the bed.

Connor didn't know what this was between them or where it had come from. Was it the island? The weather? Or was it that they were *just* as mad as one another?

I want you.

Chapter Twelve

I THINK I'VE FINALLY LOST IT.

Shaun cupped Connor's face as he kissed him. He had one leg draped over Connor's thigh, and his towel was dangerously close to falling away. He could feel the loosened knot at his waist slipping. Closing his eyes, he relaxed into Connor's hold. He let the sense of safety from being in Connor's arms wrap around him. He couldn't remember the last time he had felt so at ease, despite what had happened outside and the pool.

He ran his hand over Connor's chest. He took his time, mapping out the firm dips and rises as he neared the bundled-up towel fastened at Connor's waist. He breathed in deeply and slid his hand lower in search of entry. He grinned into the kiss as he found the gap in the towel and slipped his hand beneath the fluffy material. His fingertips brushed the heated, damp skin of Connor's thigh.

A soft sigh escaped from Connor's parted lips as Shaun moved his hand higher, gently stroking the sensitive patch of the skin of his inner thigh. Excitement clenched in Shaun's chest as Connor spread his legs slightly.

This was insane. Only days ago he had been convinced one of them would end up leaving the island with a black eye and the other with an injunction against them. But here they were, and Shaun wasn't sure what it all meant, or where it could possibly go.

Would the magic of Sapphire Cay wear off as soon as they stepped foot on the mainland?

Will I care if it does? Shaun opened his eyes and ended the kiss. He rested his chin on Connor's chest and changed the direction of his touch beneath the towel. With his fingertips, he drew lines down Connor's leg toward his knee. Then he pulled his hand free and straightened Connor's towel.

Turning his head, Shaun met Connor's curious gaze. He pursed his lips and studied Connor's face.

I will. Whatever the reasons, Shaun had feelings for Connor. He'd known there was more to those initial sparks between them when they had clashed over the story, and what would become of it. He had been attracted to Connor from the moment he set eyes on him.

"Are you okay?" Connor said. He reached over, and gently pushed back Shaun's unruly bangs. "Do you feel all right?"

Shaun pressed a kiss to Connor's chest and then rested his hand under his chin. "I'm all right. I'm just tired. I could probably do with getting some sleep."

Connor averted his eyes and nodded. "Of course." He made to move.

"You're leaving?" Shaun said and lifted his head.

"I thought..."

"Thought what?"

"I figured you were hinting at me to go."

Shaun shook his head. "God, no." He pushed himself to sit up. "I really am tired. And I was kind of hoping you'd stay."

Connor blinked and looked at the bed. "You want me to stay?"

"Yes." He looked hopefully at Connor. *Please stay.*

There was a beat, then Connor nodded. "I'd like that." He gently cupped Shaun's face and gazed into his eyes. The look in his eyes seemed to reflect Shaun's own happiness, and they met in a chaste kiss.

Shaun lay down on the bed. He rested his head on the pillow and waited, watching Connor until he was settled beside him. He smiled and rolled onto his other side. As Shaun had hoped, Connor moved close to him and draped his arm over Shaun's waist. He smiled as he sensed Connor's fingers on his back, working in soothing circles across his skin.

"Thank you for being here." Shaun closed his eyes and hugged his pillow, his smile widening as Connor ran his fingers higher and curled them through the back of his hair.

Connor pressed a kiss to Shaun's back. "I wouldn't want to be anywhere else."

I wish we didn't have to go back to reality. Did Alfie and Peter feel like this every time they had to go home? Would they always wish for more time?

With a sigh, Shaun buried his face in his pillow. He didn't want to think about the little time they had left on the Cay together.

I want more time.

A KNOCK ON THE DOOR STARTLED SHAUN FROM SLEEP, AND a voice called through the wood.

"We're calling it on the shelter," Scott said. "Get whatever you need and move down to the lobby."

Connor sat upright in bed, his hair spiky and his face creased with sleep. "How long have we been asleep?" he asked.

Shaun didn't know. He shook his head, "What about the alarm?"

"I don't know, but let's get down there."

Connor headed back to his room to grab his things, leaving Shaun to hastily get dressed alone and collect together the precious memories of Alfie and Peter. Meeting at the stairs, they went downstairs, making it to the lobby in a few minutes. Everyone was there, which made for a very crowded small space.

"We didn't hear an alarm," Connor was apologizing.

"I would have used it if you didn't unlock your door."

Connor and Shaun exchanged a look that spoke volumes.

Scott continued. "We're probably over-cautious. But radio is telling us it's a big one, and we've lost power. We may only get the tail end of it, but the hotel needs to be empty."

Lucas looked pale, but Dylan held his hand. His other hand was securely holding a lock box and Shaun imagined it was the life of the hotel in one small container. A bit like the letters and evidence of Peter and Alfie; everything important in one place.

They went through a side door off from the small reception and steps led down to a flat trap door. It reminded Shaun of disaster movies involving hurricanes, where entire families just made it in time to shut the doors as the storm passed over them. Dylan and Scott held back and encouraged the others down the now open trapdoor and into the darkness beyond. Lucas had gone first and was switching on several flashlights to illuminate the area enough for getting settled. Then he closed all of them off except the one in his hand which was sufficient to shine in the dark.

There were two rooms, one large, with several small cots, and boxes of canned goods alongside bottles of water.

"Bathroom is in there," Lucas said and waved his light to indicate the other room. "Pretty basic, only for emergencies." To the other side was a radio set-up that looked like it had come out of World War II. Shaun guessed it was a working radio, otherwise why would it still be there? He assumed it was there to contact for help if they needed it.

The men sat down, two to a cot, after Scott pulled the doors shut and bolted them closed.

"Everything will be okay," Dylan reassured them. Shaun got the impression he was encouraging Lucas under the guise of comforting everyone else. "I've done this before."

"You have?" Lucas turned to look at him.

"Few years back, I was on the island alone because the owners and Scott had gone to Marsh Harbor. We caught the tail end of the last big one, but the warning came down to get to safety. I wasn't arguing and spent six hours with my copy of the Iliad and sandwiches."

Scott cleared his throat to get everyone's attention. "Talking of that, we have food and water to last us a week if necessary, usual safety guidance applies…"

Shaun half-listened to Scott and half-thought about the history that was down in this place. Did Alfie and Peter's storm mean the two men had to hide down here? If they had, then the radio setup could well be the same as what had been here. The cots looked old as well, although the blankets were all new and wrapped in plastic. Just the idea that he was sharing this place with history was fascinating and equally a huge responsibility. Everyone had settled back to ride out the storm when Shaun thought of the fact he now had a captive audience to ask questions of. Including Dylan, who frequently avoided Shaun and his incessant curiosity.

"Do you know anything about the storms that have hit the Cay?" Shaun asked.

Dylan glanced at Lucas. "Lucas is the one with all the knowledge of storms from the accounts, lists of all the damage. He remembers all the dates and everything." Dylan sounded so proud.

Lucas dipped his eyes and Shaun could see the praise hit home. "I can't help my brain," he said with a shy smile.

"Do you want to share?" Dylan prompted.

Lucas cleared his throat. "Fifty-two was a bad one, hence the reconstruction of the dining wing, and half of the cabin accommodations." He screwed up his face in thought. "Fifty-nine there was damage to the trees area outside, but that was the year they first put the pool in so I think the hurricane cleared a lot of trees for them. Ninety-two, Hurricane Andrew was close, way too close, but the Cay pulled through that one."

"What about 1966, the year that Alfie and Peter were here?"

"Sixty-six?" Lucas did some more thinking. "Shutters," he finally said. "That was the year all the south side of the hotel took a beating, shutters, windows, all broken."

A loud crash echoed above them and the air appeared to suck upward and Shaun wasn't going to lie; he was this side of scared. "Fuck," he cursed. Then he laughed nervously, only slightly placated when Connor grasped his hand and held tight.

Another crash, this time right over their heads, and it was Dylan's turn to curse. Then he leaned into Lucas. "I'm hoping we have a budget for repairs." He was aiming for lighthearted, but Shaun could see the worry in the Dylan's eyes.

"We do, it's okay," Lucas confirmed with a smile. Then he reached over for water bottles and tossed them to each of them. He held his up. "To beating Mother Nature," he said.

They all repeated the toast and then talked about everything and nothing, as the crashing decreased then vanished, only to return again. Shaun wasn't sure when they would leave, but it seemed as if Scott had his eye on the ball. More crashing, then another period of silence before Scott cautiously unbolted the trap door. Shaun had been imagining the hotel around them in pieces, possibly even blocking them in, but somehow the hotel was not only still standing, but appeared largely undamaged.

Scott and Dylan went first out of the hotel door which had lost its shutters and glass but other than that was at least still on its hinges. There was water damage inside; Shaun didn't imagine this would be a quick clean up.

He and Connor followed the others out, and Shaun couldn't help the sadness that welled up inside him. He had hold of Mutt's lead and he let him off as soon as they reached a part that wasn't littered with glass.

"Shit," Scott muttered. "The cocktail hut is gone."

Shaun looked to where the wooden building had stood. When Scott said gone he wasn't exaggerating; the structure had vanished. All that was left was a concrete base and Shaun thought he spotted some small umbrellas; bright splashes of pink in the dark bushes.

Scott followed Dylan down to the harbor where they'd managed to tie both Liberty's down earlier. "Liberty is fine, Liberty Two is scratched to shit," Dylan called back to Lucas.

From here Shaun heard snatches of conversation but neither Dylan nor Scott appeared duly worried about the scratches.

The pool was still crammed with branches, and the sand had covered everything, including hidden glass. Shaun grabbed Mutt and tied his leash to the nearest tree in the shade. He brought him water and food then patted him a couple times. Poor thing had been bundled into the shelter and spent the entire time under Lucas and Dylan's cot, shaking.

"Kitchen is intact," Adam called from the hotel. "North side is fine."

Dylan and Scott stood next to each other arms folded across their chests, surveying the situation.

"Glass first," Dylan said. "We need to get it cleared."

"Agreed, then salvage anything we can," Lucas added.

Connor stepped forward. "What can I do?"

"I'd like to help, too," Shaun said.

Dylan opened his mouth like he was going to say something along the lines of Shaun and Connor being guests. But they weren't really, were they?

So, the six men spent the hours until dark clearing up as best they could, Scott and Dylan focusing on the windows and getting the hotel watertight. Shaun avoided the pool; let Connor and Adam deal with that one. He found a job inside the hotel helping Lucas clean up the hall and get rid of as much damage as they could.

"I guess you could get hit again this season?" Shaun said as they hefted an unusually heavy case of files up on the desk.

"Hmm?" Lucas asked. He was placing files back on shelves and concentrating hard on getting them back into whatever order they needed to be in.

"Another storm to hit Sapphire Cay? This season?"

Lucas sighed. "Yeah, probably."

"Do you ever think you and Dylan should sell up and find somewhere a bit more…safe?"

Lucas gave the suggestion consideration, just a moment or two, before placing two scarlet folders labelled as accounts, onto the shelf. "No. This place has been here a hundred years now, parts of it destroyed over the years, but we're cheating the odds here. It's home."

"I'd like to come back one day," Shaun said.

"And you'd be welcome, both of you."

"Both of us? Oh, you mean Connor. I'm sure he'll revisit one day."

"You should visit together."

Shaun gave his own small sigh. "Don't think we'll see each other after this."

Lucas leaned on his desk and crossed his hands over his chest. He looked so serious. "You want some advice?"

"Do I have a choice?" He almost knew what Lucas was going to say. Some great speech about what he saw between Shaun and Connor and what a good guy Connor was, probably with examples.

Instead, what Lucas said was, "Life is too short."

He turned back to his files and Shaun was left with the feeling he'd been given the most profound piece of advice he'd ever heard in his entire life. Life was too short. He liked Connor, and yeah, maybe when they were home, despite living in different places, maybe they could meet up and learn more about each other. As he thought long and hard, he worked on the office then went out to help Dylan.

The food was bread and anything else Adam could pull together as they worked. The oppressive air of an oncoming storm had given way to a fresh, bright day.

When Shaun fell into bed, just after ten that night, Connor climbed in next to him and they spooned until sleep.

Shaun was too exhausted to say a word. Not even to talk with Connor about why life was too short or what the two of them should do because of it.

Was there a future for them?

Chapter Thirteen

"GOOD MORNING," ADAM SAID BRIGHTLY AS CONNOR AND Shaun entered the kitchen.

Connor breathed in deeply. "Pancakes?" he guessed from the sweet batter smell. He sat next to Shaun and eyed the various syrups and bowls of fruit.

"We're using the term loosely," Scott said and sat down opposite them.

Adam brought over a pile of plates and set the table. When he got to Scott, he put the plate down with an intentional bang.

Scott blew out a breath and pulled an awkward face. "We found an old camping stove or something. Two rings, bottled gas—"

"Pretty much stuck on one burner setting," Adam interrupted and placed a large dish of pancakes down in the center of the table. He rested his hands on his hips and looked at Scott.

"That setting seemed to be charcoal." Scott leaned

forward. "So ignore any black bits." He flashed a smile as he looked innocently up at Adam.

Shaking his head, Adam pulled off his apron. "I'm going to shout for Dylan and Lucas. Feel free to make a start."

The door to the kitchen swung shut and the three men were left staring at the pancakes.

Connor pressed a hand to his stomach when it made an embarrassing sound. He eyed the food. It would be impolite to start without their hosts, right?

"So, how's the head today?" Scott asked Shaun. He threaded his fingers together and rested his elbows on the edge of the table. Connor looked at Shaun. When they'd woken up, he'd been shocked to see how bad the scratches looked the morning after the day before. If they'd been any deeper…

"I'm all right," Shaun said, on a yawn. "My face anyway, but I don't think I have a muscle left that doesn't ache."

Scott smiled in sympathy at him. "Least we got it all done. Thank you, both of you, for your help."

Shaun shrugged and yawned again. Twice in the night Connor had woken because Shaun was restless in bed. He'd explained it away as his thoughts not shutting up, and that authors had that kind of thing happen to them all the time. That was one of the things that Connor wanted to learn about Shaun. They'd showered separately, dressed apart, but they had walked down to breakfast together, Shaun yawning and Connor holding back everything he wanted to say.

"Liberty is okay to get you back tomorrow, after breakfast."

"Thank you," Shaun said immediately. Connor couldn't bring himself to do much more than nod. He really didn't want to go home. "You think we can go into the shelter and take a proper look round."

"Don't see why not," Scott said around a mouth of pancake.

"Why do we want to do that?" Connor asked at the same time.

Shaun ducked his head and a flush colored his cheek. "You're going to think it's stupid."

Connor wanted to shout that somehow everything Shaun did made him fall a little bit more, and that nothing he said was stupid, but instead all he said was, "Go on."

"I felt like there was something in there, a ghost of something, a feeling." Shaun smiled hesitantly. "Told you, it's stupid."

Connor had to wipe the hesitation from Shaun's face. "Who are we to question your inner author?" He smirked. Clearly that was the right tone to take because Shaun returned the smile and polished off his pancakes in a hurry. Even the burned bits. As they finished, Adam came back in the kitchen. Connor watched as Scott dragged Adam to straddle his lap.

"You forgiven me yet?" Scott teased. He kissed Adam gently.

Adam hooked his hands around Scott's neck. "I suppose so." They kissed again and Connor tugged Shaun out of the kitchen, both men taking mugs of hot coffee.

They walked through the hotel to the lobby and

through the side door and in a short space of time they were in the storm shelter. Both had coffee in one hand and a flashlight in the other. There was still no electricity, although Dylan had promised power by midmorning.

"The last letter we have, from Alfie, the one he never sent, talks about a storm that last summer they were here."

"And you think they were down here for that?"

"It's possible." Shaun sat on the nearest bunk directly opposite the old radio system. "I just felt it, that they were here and they sat out the storm."

Connor sat next to Shaun and curled his fingers into the soft blanket that had been left there yesterday. He wished he felt the presence of something else, some person or memory that lingered down here, but his imagination was rooted in skepticism.

"You think the radio works?" Connor stood from his perch and walked over to investigate. Technology, even old stuff like this, he could get behind. Technology was real.

"Scott told me it was a backup, and that he gave it an overhaul a few months back."

Connor slid into the small chair in front of it and picked up the handset turning it over in his hands before putting back. The whole rig, large, black and mysterious in this light, stood on a metal table and Connor ran his fingers over the edge. He desperately wanted to feel like Shaun did; like there was a connection in this room. All he felt was cold metal, a notch and bump or two in the otherwise smooth surface, then the edge.

Idly he repeated the stroke as he listened to Shaun speak. "I'm going to have to fill in with my feelings about what happened in the storm," Shaun explained. "Give the reader a feel for what this goodbye meant to them. Alfie was dying, Peter knew that, and these were their last few weeks."

Shaun came up behind him but didn't touch him; Connor leaned back in the chair a little and rested the back of his head on Shaun's stomach. Shaun rested his hands firmly on Connor's shoulders.

"Life is too short," Shaun murmured.

Connor stilled the movement of his hands on the last notch before the left corner and traced the pattern of it. "Life is too short."

"I was thinking…."

"About?"

"Us meeting up when we get back to the mainland when this is all over. I could visit with Annalisa, and try and talk your grandfather around to Annalisa's way of thinking. I could show them I mean to do right by Alfie and Peter."

Connor was disappointed. "Is that the only reason you want to meet up?"

Shaun moved his hands, fingers under the fabric of Connor's shirt on the back of his neck. "No," he paused a little longer. "I like you. A lot. I was thinking we could maybe date, and see how it goes?"

"I'd like that," Connor said. He moved in the chair, using his hands on the table as leverage and made to stand up, only to catch his board shorts on the desk itself and stumble into Shaun's arms. Connor cursed as he heard material rip, but the curse turned to laughter as Shaun hauled him up, cradled his face, and angled for a kiss.

They kissed in the semidarkness for a long time; completely alone and falling into the sensation together.

"We should take this outside," Connor finally managed to get a word in. With a pout of disapproval, Shaun finally let him go. Together they disentangled material from the desk but it wasn't coming free.

"You need to take them off," Shaun suggested.

"I'm wearing nothing under them," Connor said. To which Shaun pulled him in for more kissing, with added hands down board shorts and Connor close to coming in this dark room. This time it was Shaun who stepped back.

"Come on," he said, falling to his knees. Connor's chest tightened at the thought of a blow job in here. He was, to put it mildly, a bit disappointed when Shaun set about freeing the material with the aid of a flashlight. "There's something here," he said. "Hang on, you're caught on…got it…no…shuffle this way a bit."

Connor did as he was told, moved slightly to his right. "Is that okay?"

"Fuck," Shaun cursed. "You'll never believe… Oh, shit."

"What?" Connor couldn't help sounding worried. He hadn't felt blood but maybe he was actually stuck fast and they'd need Scott or Dylan to come down with a blowtorch. His hard-on shriveled at the thought of a blowtorch near his groin.

Shaun yanked hard and Connor stumbled free, the torn material flapping on his thigh.

"Look," Shaun said. He held up what looked like a small tin, but Connor couldn't make out detail. Shaun hadn't stood, so Connor went to a crouch at his side.

"What is it?"

"I don't know, it was riveted to the base of this thing. Do you think it's Alfie and Peter's?"

"We should get it out into the light and have a look."

They climbed up out of the shelter and Connor closed the doors. They made their way out to sunshine and clear blue skies and blinked at the change in light. By unspoken agreement, they moved to the shade of the closest palm tree and sat on the sand at its base. Shaun placed the box in between them. Made of metal, it was rusting at one corner and Connor hoped to hell, if there was something inside it, the contents weren't ruined. He could just make out the brand as an old tobacco company and the box itself was little more than six inches by four.

"Should we open it?" Shaun asked. He tapped it. "It isn't our property."

Connor scrambled to stand. "Wait there."

He went straight to the office. Lucas was sitting at one desk, Dylan on his knees under the other desk cursing a blue streak.

"Can I show you something? We found it in the storm shelter."

Dylan sat up and smacked his head on the bottom of the desk, cursed, then scrambled out from under it. "What?" he asked. Lucas had already stood up.

"Some kind of container, or something, we thought it should be you who open it."

The three men went outside. They joined Shaun, all sitting cross-legged in a circle around the tin on the ground.

"It's not very big." Lucas sounded disappointed. "Not as big as the one we found, anyway."

"Do you think it's theirs?" Dylan asked.

Shaun answered, "I don't know. But I guess we should open it?"

Dylan reached out and picked it up, examining the sides, scraping at the rust with his fingernail. He attempted to pry off the lid but it wouldn't budge, so he pulled out a penknife and began to press it around each side. Slowly and surely the top began to move, and finally with the rasp of metal on metal, the lid fell off.

Connor leaned in, the same as everyone else. Inside were three pieces of folded paper.

Dylan opened the top one and gasped; a beautifully drawn pencil sketch of two men hugging each other. One of them was clearly Peter, the other was Alfie, but he looked a lot skinnier than the photos from the forties. In the corner was the same small shell as was on all the letters from back then, but next to it was initials and what Connor assumed was the year. PF '66.

"It was Peter who was the artist," Connor said. He had hoped he was right to believe the artwork was Peter's, now knowing the truth, the idea of someone in his family tree being so talented at art blew him away.

"Seems like he was," Dylan commented. He peered closer at the drawing then passed it round.

When it reached Connor, he held it carefully by the corner. Finally, he understood what Shaun had meant about a connection. Because right here, was his great-great-uncle who had sketched something that was pure love. He swallowed the emotion that choked his throat. Why didn't Peter take the drawing home with him? Why leave it here?

"They closed the circle with this," Shaun whispered. "The photos were here, and they wanted to leave their mark. They must have been in the shelter and seen somewhere that could remain untouched."

Dylan unfolded the next bit of paper; he scanned it then cleared his throat. "My dearest darling Peter, I leave you with a great sadness that I know you will mourn my passing. Remember me, and carry me in your heart, and know I am waiting for you. Forever, Alfie." Dylan swallowed audibly and passed the note directly to Shaun, like the connection was his to have first.

Then he opened the second note, a looser scrawl, familiar from the letters they already had, written by Peter.

"To the other half of my heart, Alfie," Dylan began. "Yours. Always." He passed that note to Connor, who took it reverently.

Always.

Yours.

He and Shaun held hands on the sand at that moment. They gripped tight and something was there. The gentle wash of memories and the almost unbelievable grief that came with knowing this was Alfie and Peter's last meeting.

And with hands held, and letters from the past, a connection was made.

THEY LEFT THE ISLAND THE NEXT MORNING. NEITHER Connor nor Shaun had much sleep in the bank; they'd spent most of the night talking to Lucas and Dylan. Connor could listen to Shaun talk about his book all day. He was eloquent and the story he was creating in his mind was so very personal to everyone. He couldn't wait to read it.

They shared a flight to Miami and held hands the entire way. They spoke about the island and the men whose lives were part of theirs. But when they reached Miami, Connor realized he didn't even know where Shaun lived.

"Where does your connection take you?" Connor asked as they waited for their bags.

"Where does yours?" Shaun answered with a question of his own.

"New York." He would be back in the office tomorrow. Back to reality.

Connor waited for Shaun to give him an answer, but their bags arrived, and their attention turned to that instead.

They made their way out of arrivals and Connor checked his open return. It may well be hugely expensive to have an open return, but he hadn't had any idea when he was going back. "So, where are you heading?"

Shaun still didn't answer. And this was getting awkward. Finally, he pushed back his shoulders. "There's no shame in not having a permanent place to stay," he began. "I'm creative and authors needed to explore their world."

"I guess," Connor said. Who was Shaun trying to convince?

Shaun sighed. "That's not exactly true," he admitted. "It's like this. I was in London for a long time. Then I came home to help Dad clear out Grandad's house a little way outside Seattle. I was only renting in London, so now I guess I'm going back to Dad's." His tone was a little defiant. Like he was daring Connor to ask why he didn't have a place to go that was his own.

"Come to mine," Connor blurted. "I have this apartment, four bedrooms, you could stay there with me, and we could…"

"What, Connor? What could we do?" Shaun tilted his head a little as he said it. He looked tired, but at the same time there was hope in his eyes.

Suddenly exploring the world seemed like an option Shaun could be happy to shelve for a while. Connor had to make him see that he wanted a space that was *theirs*. But did Shaun think this was just out of pity? Or did Shaun still feel some of that magic from the island, the same as Connor did?

"We could date," Connor said softly. "And I could help you with the book."

Shaun appeared to consider the offer, then nodded. "Dating is good."

And right there, in the middle of the airport, with humanity streaming around them, Connor dropped his bags and pulled Shaun close and kissed him so thoroughly that only a lack of breath pushed them apart. Shaun looked a little dazed.

"You think you could fall for me? Like I'm falling for you?" Connor asked softly.

Shaun blinked at him, a soft smile on his kiss-swollen lips. "Already am," he said.

And so they kissed again.

Chapter Fourteen

A WHOLE WEEK HAD PASSED SINCE THE KISS IN THE airport. True to his word Connor had given Shaun his own room, which was like a freaking palace. A huge king-sized bed with room all the way around it, an attached bathroom with two sinks, a tub, and a shower. It was like he was staying in a million-star hotel.

Then there was the food. Connor liked to cook, and Shaun was happy to watch after explaining how crap he was at cooking. Connor created dinners which they ate in the small dining room with views over the city, and Shaun tidied everything away. They were a team. There was money in Connor's life, but he wasn't affected by it. He had the best of everything, but he worked long hours for the French Foundation and Shaun had plenty of down time with his trusty laptop and was making headway with the plans for the book. He'd spoken to his publisher who wanted to see the outlines for the remaining chapters and who had authorized an advance. While not being millions, the amount was certainly enough for Shaun to offer to pay rent and to have some money to live on for the next year.

Of course, Connor turned him down, but Shaun had at least made the offer and felt better for it. The seven days since leaving the Cay had been quiet and relaxed, but the tension between Shaun and Connor was palpable. They kissed. A lot. In fact, every chance they got they kissed and they'd exchanged mutual handjobs, and even one very memorable exchange of blow jobs in Connor's shower, which was as big as a small living room.

But actually sharing a room? Sleeping together? Somehow that wasn't happening and Shaun really wanted that to happen. He dug around in the kitchen, pulled out the ingredients for lasagna and had the meal in the oven with wine chilling in the fridge, all ready for when Connor came through the door.

Knowing it would be at least thirty minutes he pulled out the photos of Peter and Alfie and arranged them on the table. He had this idea for a cover, a montage of the pictures, hiding any naked bits under others. He arranged them, but as he looked at them, he realized something was missing. Sliding in the hand-drawn sketch he chose one photo of a smiling Peter, another of Alfie grinning up at the camera and placed them next to the drawing.

"That looks perfect," Connor said from behind him. Shaun nearly hit the roof in shock and whirled to face Connor.

"You scared the shit out of me," he announced.

Connor kissed his hand and finally Shaun relaxed against him.

"I've had the day from hell," Connor said on a yawn. He sniffed the air appreciatively. "You cooked?"

"You know I don't do that," Shaun admitted. "I followed the instructions on the lasagna sheets and bought jars of stuff from the deli. There's wine in the fridge."

"Sounds like cooking to me. And wine I need."

They ate and drank as Connor explained about his day.

"Oscar came in, demanded first sight of the manuscript, blustering and getting in everyone's way. And you'll never guess who turned up about five minutes later?"

"Who?"

"Annalisa."

"Did the shit hit the fan?"

"Big time. Incidentally, she's asked us to visit this weekend. She said I should bring my boyfriend over so she could see who's got me all mixed up."

Shaun filed that comment away for later. Boyfriend sounded nice. "What did she say to Oscar?"

"She cut him dead, said no one cared to get offended about a love story that ended fifty years ago. Then when he got all up in her face, she said he was an idiot and that if you didn't publish the book she would tell the story of what she knew herself."

Shaun felt relief. At least he had Annalisa on his side. Maybe she would agree to an interview after their informal meet up.

"Anyway, she said she'd love to give you some quotes, tell you what it was like back then. If that helps anyway."

"Wow," Shaun was lost for words.

"So…" Connor pushed away his empty plate. "That

brings me to the other thing."

"The other what?"

"At work. I was talking to Miriam, you know my PA, the one who let you past the door right when we first met."

"I remember her."

"She was asking about you. She said I had a stupid smile on my face. Which of course, meant I had to consciously not smile all day. That is hard when I'm thinking about how much I feel for you."

The sentence was so long and said all on one breath. "You think about me?"

Connor nodded. "All day, every moment I can, your hopeless romanticism, your ability to burn water, your smile, your laugh, the way you sleep. Talking of that, I was thinking maybe tonight we could…sleep…y'know…"

"What?" Shaun blinked at Connor. He wasn't following, then just as quickly the words made sense. "I thought you'd never ask," Shaun said. He held out a hand and stood. "Let's start now."

Connor pulled them to a stop. "It's only been two weeks. But is it too early to…"

Shaun took a leap into the unknown. "I'm falling in love with you."

"Oh. Thank God for that," Connor said. "I fell for you the minute my feet touched Sapphire Cay."

Shaun pressed a soft kiss to Connor's lips, and simply said two words. "Island magic."

Eleven months later

. . .

THE BOXES SAT IN A NICE EVEN LINE, STRETCHING FROM the door of the apartment and into the start of the kitchen.

"How many did they send?" Connor asked. He crouched next to the nearest box and checked the label. "One of ten? And how many are in each box?"

Shaun pulled the tape from the box nearest to him and peered inside at the spines of the hardbacks of Peter and Alfie's story. "Fifteen? Twenty?" he offered.

"To give away?"

"Yeah, I guess."

The last year had been full of deadlines and agreements and publishing nightmares and a whole lot of love between two men brought together by an old love. To have the boxes sitting here, with *his* book in them, was the full stop in this complicated happy paragraph of his life.

"Are you sending one to the Cay?"

Shaun pulled out a copy and held it balanced on one palm. He'd seen mockups of the book before, the artwork, the sleeve, the dedication, the words inside. But this was real. The cover was perfect, the inside was faultless, the dedication heartfelt and emotional. He carried a copy to the table and picked up a pen. With little thought to what he was writing he wrote the first words that came to mind, then pushed the book to one side.

"I'll get it couriered tomorrow," he said.

Connor gathered him into a hug. "I'm so proud of you."

Shaun hugged back. "I love you."

"I love you, too."

"Always?"

"Always."

Chapter Fifteen

LUCAS CROSSED HIS ANKLES AND LAY BACK ON THE SAND. He stared up at the hazy sky through his sunglasses.

Another season done.

The year had flown by, and Lucas didn't like how quickly time was getting away from them. How was he supposed to enjoy forever here on the island with his incredible husband, if forever had hit fast-forward?

Closing his eyes, Lucas idly stroked his hand over Mutt's belly. The dog was lying beside him under one of the patio parasols, worn out from playing fetch with a Frisbee. Mutt made a small noise as he shifted his body, arching his belly into Lucas's hand, making Lucas smile.

The sound of his cell phone interrupted the peaceful moment. Lucas opened his eyes briefly to answer the call.

"Hello," he said. He settled back on the rolled-up towel under his head. Mutt barked disapprovingly, and Lucas swapped the phone to his other hand. "Hello."

"Lucas, it's me." There was no mistaking Edward's to-the-point tone.

Lucas yawned as he scratched circles through Mutt's coat. "Hey, Edward. Everything okay?" With the final wedding of the season completed to perfection, Edward had headed back to Miami with Jamie. As far as Lucas was concerned, he hadn't expected to hear from the wedding planner until the few weeks in the run-up to the first wedding of next season. Edward would phone, email, phone again, and send three more emails informing them of delivery dates and menus and any of the other weird and wonderful requests Edward's clients happened to make.

"Okay? Of course everything's okay. I am back in Miami, the sun is shining, and I am up to my elbows in color swatches for next year's biggest wedding. I bet you can't guess whose?"

"Dylan owes me fifty bucks."

"What?" Edward's voice rose a little at the end of the word. "What are you talking about?"

"Well, Jamie's asked you to marry him, right?" Lucas had made the bet with Dylan after their own wedding as to who was likely to get married first out of Scott and Edward. Dylan had insisted Scott was the most likely to do something so ridiculously impulsive, probably on a whim in some foreign country. Lucas had been sure Edward and Jamie would be the ones to do it properly, to want to settle down, and have it all official.

There was a long silence.

"Edward?"

"Why would you say that?" Edward's voice was edged with suspicion. "Has Jamie said something? He's been hanging out with you and Dylan too much hasn't he? He's going to ask me. I thought he was happy with what we had. He said he was okay. He said he was okay to wait if I wasn't sure. I don't know if I want to get married. I'm going to have to say yes, aren't I? Then I'll be left to plan everything. You know what he's like. I don't think I can handle the stress."

"Whoa." Lucas opened his eyes. "What? So Jamie hasn't asked you?"

"No. But he's going to, isn't he? Oh oh."

Lucas imagined Edward blowing out his cheeks with each panicked breath he took. "Just chill out. My mistake. He isn't going to ask you."

"Huh? You promise?" The relief behind Edward's words was clear as day.

Pursing his lips, Lucas debated if he could make that promise. "Erm, sure, I guess. Not anytime soon anyway."

"Oh. My. God. What are you trying to do to me?"

"I just assumed. You said about a big wedding and were making me guess. I figured this was your way of saying you were engaged." Lucas pushed himself to sit up. "Sorry?"

"Useless. I was making you guess because I, my dear, have finally made it. I only went and bagged myself a celebrity wedding. A very handsome movie star whose name I can't tell you. I figured by making you guess I could make some sort of grunty noise and you'd figure it all out." He sighed loudly down the phone. "You've probably never heard of him anyway. You have island brain."

Island brain?

"Erm, remember who pays your wages."

"Dylan." Edward chuckled, clearly thinking himself

funny. "Anyway, I meant you have your own little paradise that you live in with one of the most perfect men I know. I doubt drooling over the back catalogue of action movies this guy's been in is really high on your priority list."

Nice save.

"So you want me to guess?" Lucas checked.

Edward tutted. "Nope. You've ruined my moment. There's no point playing now."

"Sorry, I guess?" Lucas glanced to the pier, a smile spreading across his face as he noticed Liberty Two wasn't far out. "Was there anything else you wanted?"

"No. That was it. What are you doing anyway?"

"Waiting for Dylan. He was dropping the last of our guests back at Marsh Harbor."

"And waiting for him to get back so you can partake in a little quality time, just the two of you?"

Lucas leaned forward and scratched Mutt's head. He pushed the water bowl a little closer. "There you go, lazy," he said in a low voice to Mutt. He shifted his attention back to the call. "If by quality time you mean catching up on some sleep, then yeah." He laughed. The end of the season was like some massive comedown from all the stress and adrenaline of keeping Sapphire Cay running like the well-oiled machine he and Dylan strived for it to be for their guests.

"Well, you'd have earned it."

"Thanks."

"Anyway, I'd best get on. I'm sure you have plenty to do too."

Lucas wriggled his toes beneath the cool sand shaded

by the umbrella. "Oh, yeah. I have really important things I need to do. I should get right on those."

"You're sitting by the pool with a cocktail aren't you?"

Shaking his head as he spoke, Lucas said, "Nope. I am nowhere near the pool."

Liberty Two was at the pier, and Dylan was in sight.

"Enjoy the time off," Edward said.

"Thanks. Say hi to Jamie for us."

"Will do. Bye."

"Bye." Lucas hung up and placed his cell on the blanket in the shade. Bringing up his knees, he rested his folded arms on them and waited as Dylan did his thing and secured the boat.

His gaze drifted to his hand and the wedding band on his finger. With a smile, he twisted it slightly, pushing it up to his knuckle to reveal the untanned strip of skin.

They had been husband and husband for almost fifteen months. Already they'd celebrated their one-year anniversary. How crazy did that sound? But also how perfect?

Bloody perfect. Lucas grinned as he channeled his inner Edward. He slid his sunglasses down his nose and watched Dylan cross the sand toward him. The view was incredible, as it always was. Just as amazing as that very first time he'd set eyes on Dylan at the harbor side. He quirked his eyebrow at the memory and studied Dylan. It was just like that first time—his tanned skin, his dark hair with sun bleached blond streaks, his cut-off tee putting his muscular arms on show. Lucas snorted a laugh. Dylan was wearing the same faded pink tee he had that very first time. The T-shirt might be a little more worn and weathered since that first time, but it still encompassed everything Lucas had loved in Dylan. His free spirit, and what he offered Lucas—freedom, love, and maybe even his life.

"I got seaweed on my face or something?" Dylan stopped in front of Lucas. He looked down and ran his tongue around his teeth.

"Just looking," Lucas said. He kicked some sand up at Dylan, hitting him on the shin. His gaze fell to a bound package in Dylan's hands. It didn't look like supplies and seemed strangely old-fashioned wrapped in brown paper and a piece of string around it. "What's that?"

"I don't know. It was waiting at the post office. It's addressed to us both."

"Any return address?"

Dylan smiled and sat down on the sand. "The French Foundation offices in New York."

Lucas tilted his head as he looked at the package. Something else he couldn't believe had really been a year ago. "Peter and Alfie," he said softly.

They hadn't heard from Connor or Shaun in months, not since Shaun sent them an email to let them know he had the backing of Annalisa and the French family, and the book would be published.

"That's what I figured." Dylan straightened out his legs and rested the package in his lap. It took him a moment, but he eventually freed the package from the loop of string. Then he handed it to Lucas. "You do it."

Lucas took the parcel. He ran his hands around the neatly folded paper. Part of him wanted to rip it open, like a kid at Christmas and get to the good stuff inside. Another part wanted to give the moment, and Alfie and Peter, the respect they deserved.

Finding a space along the fold that hadn't been taped down, Lucas carefully picked at it until he was able to pull the strip away. He folded back the edges and reached inside.

"Let's do it together," he said, having pulled the cardboard box to the side of the paper. He moved his hand to one side, making space for Dylan's. Together they pulled the box free. They stared at it in silence for a moment, until Dylan took the initiative and unfastened the tab, and opened the box.

"One more layer," Dylan said and lifted the bubble-wrapped book from the box. He handed it to Lucas like they were in some game of pass the parcel and it was now Lucas's turn to remove a layer. Dylan folded the paper and string inside the box and placed it on the sand.

The book felt heavy in Lucas's hands. It was overwhelming to think his home was part of some great love story—a story he was now holding in his hands.

After taking a breath, Lucas finished unwrapping the book. "Wow," he said. He rested his hand on the glossy sleeve. "That's them." Two thirds of the cover was made up of overlapping photographs of Peter and Alfie, lying on a background of some of the handwritten letters, small snippets of love-filled words visible, and one of Peter's sketches.

"It beautiful," Dylan stated.

"They deserved beautiful." He flipped the book over and gazed over the words on the back—a love story; two men separated by war, responsibility, the law; a second chance. Lucas turned the book in his hands and stared at the top photograph. Though aged over the years, there was no mistaking the happiness on both men's faces. Lucas couldn't imagine having lived in a time where he wouldn't have been able to be with the person he loved. Sure, Peter might have loved Alfie every single day for all those years, but to never be able to show their love to the world? That must have been heartbreaking.

Lucas smiled when Dylan rested his hand over his. He looked at his husband. He was so grateful for Dylan, for Sapphire Cay. He kissed Dylan.

"What was that for?"

"Just because."

Dylan pressed a kiss to Lucas's lips. "Just because," he repeated and pulled away his hand.

Lucas opened the book. His heart swelled with pride at the scrawled message inside.

THANK YOU FOR THE PART YOU BOTH PLAYED IN MAKING THIS book a reality. Thank you for giving Peter and Alfie their happy ending.

Life is too short, and we must follow our hearts when we can. So again, I thank you and the magic of your island for guiding mine and Connor's hearts to each other.

S

BENEATH THE NOTE, SHAUN HAD DRAWN A SIMPLE SKETCH of a scallop shell.

"Like on the letters." Lucas closed the book. He turned

and looked at Dylan. Life was too short, and he had nearly found that out the hard way. "Any regrets?" he asked.

"About what?"

Lucas wrapped his hand around Dylan's wrist. He turned over Dylan's arm and circled his thumb over Dylan's sun tattoo. "About us? About giving up this?" He tapped his thumb against the tattoo. "Following the sun?"

"I gave it up for you. I don't regret that." He moved closer, gently running his hand through the side of Lucas's hair. He met Lucas's gaze. Dylan's eyes seemed a shade darker than the usual cool blue. "And if I had that time back to choose again, I would choose you. Every. Single. Time." He punctuated his words with kisses and wrapped his hand around the back of Lucas's neck.

You are my sun.

"I love you," Lucas whispered on Dylan's lips. He closed his eyes and kissed Dylan again, slow and open-mouthed.

Always.

"I love you, too," Dylan said between kisses.

Forever.

HAVE YOU READ OUR BOYFRIEND FOR HIRE SERIES?

Fake Boyfriends

Have you read the Boyfriend for Hire books?

It only takes one week to fall into bed, but will Darcy and Adrian commit to a lifetime of love?

Hired to act the part of a devoted boyfriend to a wealthy socialite is just another day in the office for Darcy.

He's a professional and needs to keep his head in the game, but it throws him for a loop when he's attracted to his date's brother. Particularly when falling for the stubborn Adrian might lead to him losing the job he loves.

Adrian has been as unlucky in love as his sister, but the insane plan of hiring a fake boyfriend is chaos waiting to happen, and he refuses to endorse the move. Acting on the burning temptation for the sexy fake boyfriend leads to a love he can't ignore, even if Darcy's whispers feel as if they could be lies.

It only takes one week to fall into bed, but will Darcy and Adrian commit to a lifetime of love?

Boyfriends for Hire (with Meredith Russell)

Darcy | Kaden | Gideon | Jared | *Felix* (Fall, 2021)

Boyfriends for Hire

Boyfriends For Hire

1. <u>Darcy</u>
2. <u>Kaden</u>
3. Gideon
4. Jared
5. Felix
6. Caleb

Standalone Christmas

- <u>The Road to Frosty Hollow</u>

Also from RJ & Meredith

Standalone Christmas

- <u>The Road to Frosty Hollow</u>

Free Reads

- Stronger Together

Meet RJ Scott

RJ discovered romance in books at a very young age and realized that if there wasn't romance on the page, she could create it in her head. With over one hundred and fifty books published, she is a full time author of gay romance.

She lives and works out of her home in the beautiful English countryside, spends her spare time reading, watching films, and enjoying time with her family.

The last time she had a week's break from writing she didn't like it one little bit and has yet to meet a box of chocolates she couldn't defeat.

www.rjscott.co.uk | rj@rjscott.co.uk

NEWSLETTER - rjscott.co.uk/rjnews

facebook.com/author.rjscott

instagram.com/rjscott_author

amazon.com/author/rj-scott

bookbub.com/authors/rj-scott

goodreads.com/rjscott

patreon.com/RJScott

Meet Meredith Russell

Meredith Russell lives in the heart of England. An avid fan of many story genres, she enjoys nothing less than a happy ending. She believes in heroes and romance and strives to reflect this in her writing. Sharing her imagination and passion for stories and characters is a dream Meredith is excited to turn into reality.

www.meredithrussell.co.uk
meredithrussell666@gmail.com

facebook.com/meredithrussellauthor
x.com/MeredithRAuthor
instagram.com/miss_meredith_r